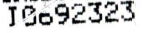

Stories of Enchantment:

Twelve Fairy Tale Sonnets

STORIES OF ENCHANTMENT

Text Copyright 2016 by Jessa Rose Sexton
Illustration Copyright 2016 by Rehanna Mae Grant
ISBN: 978-0-9966962-5-8

Written by Jessa R. Sexton
Illustrations by Rehanna Mae Grant
Final book preparation by Whitnee Clinard

Published by
Hilliard Press
a division of
The Hilliard Institute for Educational Wellness

Franklin, Tennessee
Oxford, England

www.hilliardinstitute.com

Stories of Enchantment:

TWELVE FAIRY TALE SONNETS

Written by Jessa R. Sexton
Illustrated by Rehanna Mae Grant

Dedication

for Ambrosia (though some call her Amber), my sounding board through this entire project,

for my parents, who taught me the splendor of stories and enchantment,

and for my mentors, ladies who show me what real strength, grace, and beauty are: my mum, Lisa Carr, Carolyn Davis, Dottie Frye, Esheron McKay, Gloria Merritt, and Pam Sekulow.

-JRS

To my mom, for being my strength and always believing in me.

-RMG

Special Thanks

I'd like to thank my *sonnet consultants*—
Amber Bartlett, K. Mark Hilliard, Rosemary J.
Hilliard, Rebecca Mayes, Heidi Sue Treibel,
and David Woodfine.

Also, my never-ending thanks goes to Rehanna
for creating illustrations even my dreams couldn't
have drawn and to Whitnee who always knows
what I want even when I don't.

-JRS

Table of Contents

Forward

Cinderella

Hansel and Gretel

Snow White

Pyramus and Thisbe

Little Red Riding Hood

The Mermaid

Thumbelina

The Happy Prince

The Princess and the Pea

The Maiden in the Tower

Silver-Hair and Those Three Bears

Sleeping Beauty

Afterword: A Note on Sonnets

Bibliography

About the Author

About the Illustrator

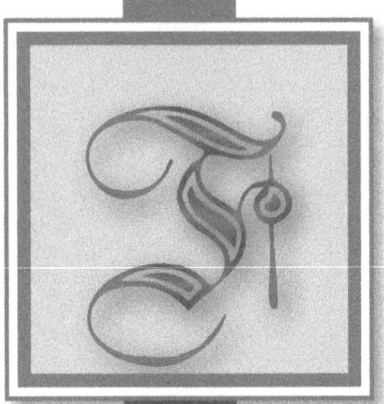

ORWARD

In 2015, I had the idea to put fairy tales into sonnet format: condensing an entire story into fourteen structured lines. I don't remember my exact inspiration. I've adored sonnets for years. The girl who used to balk at poem forms now finds this particular form the best way to sort out and better ponder her thought processes.

Because of my intimate research through that year, I could now talk forever to anyone who would listen about the different versions and changes I discovered, the symbols and meanings I considered, the commentaries and essays I studied. Instead of filling this entire book with my enthusiastic ramblings, I've decided to condense my findings into a brief three parts below as well as a couple of paragraphs after each fairy tale. The three elements I want to share now are the often-presence of birds, the roles of woman, and the purpose of fairy tales themselves. Again, this isn't meant to be an exhaustive telling of everything I've discovered (You are welcome, and/or I'll write that book another time.), but just a whetting of your own appetite, hopefully, to begin your own journey into the beautiful world of fairy tales.

Birds

Birds have a solid role in many fairy tales. They come to Cinderella's aid time and again, even to the point of plucking out the eyes of her step-relatives. Thumbelina saves a swallow who, in turn, saves her from marrying the mole king. The bird in "The Happy Prince" is a main character, helping the prince show kindness to those in need (needs he never saw when he was alive), loving the prince too dearly to desert him, and sharing an eternal reward with the prince for their selflessness.

Critic Bruno Bettelheim points out that birds bring both harm and help in "Hansel and Gretel," though his interpretation is that even the harmful actions are for the good of the two children in the end: "birds eat the bread crumbs and thus prevent the children from returning home without first meeting their great adventure. It is also a bird which guides Hansel and Gretel to the gingerbread house, and thanks only to another bird do they manage to get back home" (162).

Though they have a trial when facing the witch, "the birds must have known that it is preferable" for these siblings to "risk facing the dangers of the world" instead of returning home before they "gain their reward" (163), which isn't just emotional or mental but also monetary: they stand up to a witch and steal her treasure; they will never be hungry again, and their family (minus their stepmother who conveniently dies while they are gone) can be reunited without fear for the future. If the birds lead the reader on a journey to the moral, then the lesson of this story isn't to avoid taking risks or eating a stranger's house, but rather to meet challenges and know what is gained in

the process will outweigh what could be
lost.

WOMEN

The second important figures or symbols in
fairy tales are women. Not only has the princess
figure developed largely from fairy tales, but
the evil old woman has as well. Is this dueling
female representation supposed to be confusing?

As Harvard folklore and mythology professor
Maria Tatar points out, though the old women
in these stories are often "nags, witches, evil
stepmothers, cannibals, ogres," which is "quite
dreadful" (and, really, the complete opposite of
their innocent, beautiful counterparts), they "are
also powerful—they're often the ones who can
work magic" (qtd. in Blair). In fact, the princess
figure, or the one considered a heroine, is often
forlorn and even weak in some way—being
saved by a man or having life happen to her,
rather than being strong and assertive. And yet
that is the female we are supposed to sympathize
with and wish to be, not the woman who goes
out and makes things happen (though, of course,
those things she is making happen are envy-
inspired murders). Women cannot win,
huh?

Yet, they do—because little Gretel saves her brother with her wit; Silver-hair ransacks the home of three bears and lives to tell about it; and the Princess and the Pea survives one sleepless night and wins over the hearts of the prince and her future in-laws.

Purpose

Which brings me to my next topic. I'd never truly contemplated the purpose of fairy tales. In a basic, economic sense, Michael Newton explains, "Fairy tales were not merely ethereal properties, they were also a business, and afforded to writers a dual market of children and adults, as well as a means to position themselves as a particular kind of writer" (xii). British authors in the Victorian times used fairy tales as a means of telling an "artful version of supposedly naïve folk art" (xii). Indeed, "in the Victorian literary fairy tale, folklore becomes the root of a literary art" (xiv). And the art of writing a fairy tale included delving back into its history, sifting through the various versions, and learning about the cultures hidden in those stories.

But there is more to the fairy tale than the marketability or the artistic challenge in its writing and publishing. Elisabeth Blair says, "The point of these ancient tales, no matter what continent they come from, may have been to scare children into behaving." Perhaps. Though, most of the older versions I read didn't seem to be written for children. J.R.R. Tolkien himself pointed out that there isn't always a correlation between fairy tales and children. As Newton explains, "Ideas of the childlike, and of the trust, open-heartedness, and wonder once found in the child infiltrated critics' and writers' views of the form. For adults, reading fairy tales extended a route back into the childhood they had lost, or retained merely fitfully" (xvi).

The more I read the stories, the more I thought: sometimes a story is a story; a character is a character (as "stock" or flat as she may seem). Sometimes the process of crafting–of telling the tale–is part of the purpose itself. Sometimes a story is an escape, a reminder of the need to break from reality periodically. And sometimes the passing down of a story, because it has been given to you, is purpose enough.

So maybe fairy tales try to share a lesson, but the bigger lesson I gained from these stories is that the world isn't always explainable, and enchantment is worth sharing.

The Rehanna Mae

Cinderella

The little birds can hear you cry and catch
your tears till they run dry; your mother's gone,
your dad poorly replaced her. But hold on,
Ella, keep your dreams; there is light attached,
though dark it seems, and evil is no match
for limitless love. The little birds, drawn
to your sad plight, will help you clean till dawn
breaks bright; hearing your wish, with swift dispatch,
they'll return and soon replace that patched dress
with a golden one well suited for a queen.
When you romance the prince, and leave your shoe—
when he searches the kingdom for you; just
know your little birds are apt at the scene
to pluck out the mean of those who hurt you.

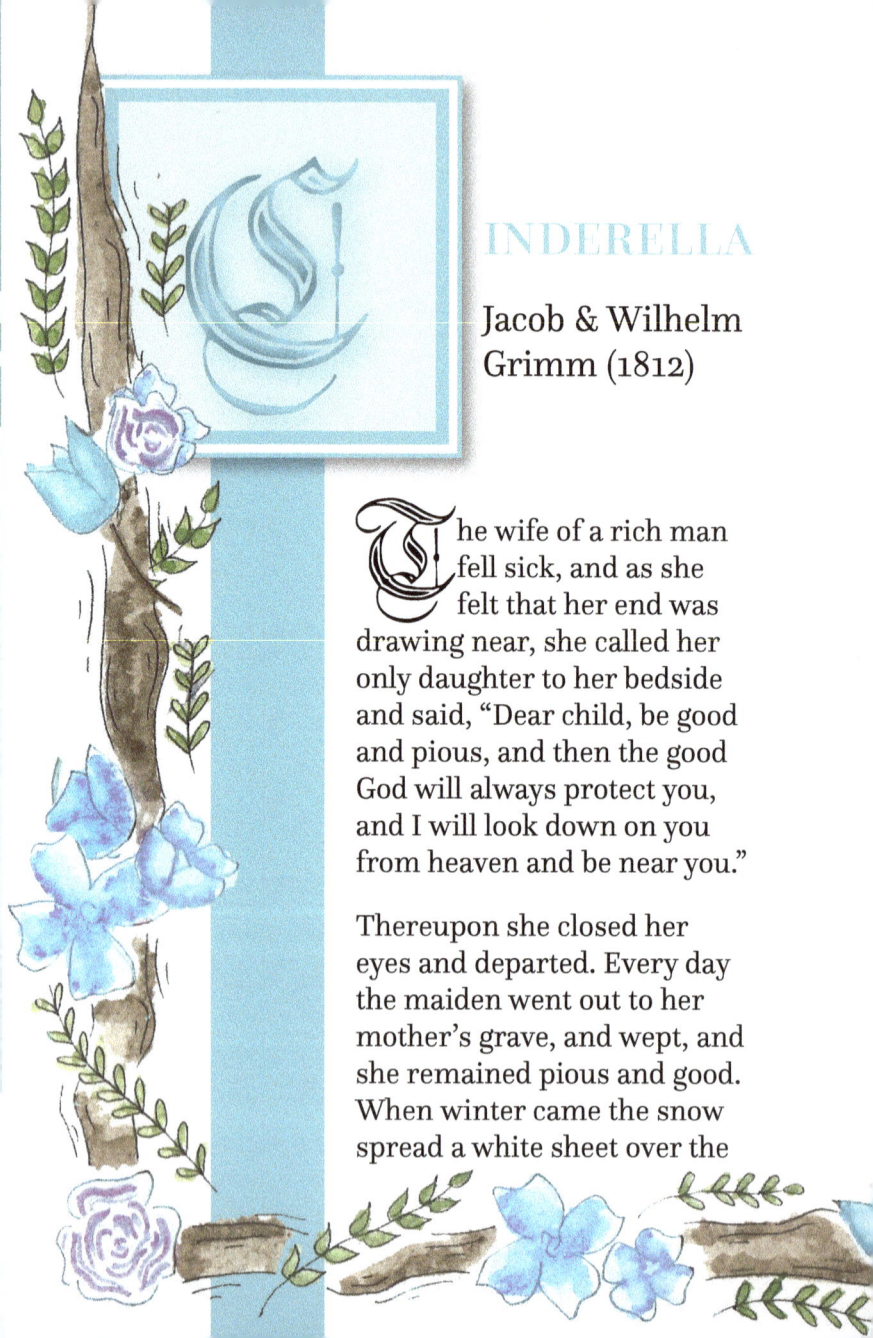

CINDERELLA

Jacob & Wilhelm Grimm (1812)

The wife of a rich man fell sick, and as she felt that her end was drawing near, she called her only daughter to her bedside and said, "Dear child, be good and pious, and then the good God will always protect you, and I will look down on you from heaven and be near you."

Thereupon she closed her eyes and departed. Every day the maiden went out to her mother's grave, and wept, and she remained pious and good. When winter came the snow spread a white sheet over the grave, and by the time the spring sun had drawn it off again, the man had taken another wife.

The woman had brought with her into the house two daughters, who were beautiful and fair of face, but vile and black of heart. Now began a bad time for the poor step-child. "Is the stupid goose to sit in the parlor with us," they said. "He who wants to eat bread must earn it. Out with the kitchen-wench." They took her pretty clothes away from her, put an old grey bedgown on her, and gave her wooden shoes.

"Just look at the proud princess, how decked out she is," they cried, and laughed, and led her into the kitchen. There she had to do hard work from morning till night, get up before daybreak, carry water, light fires, cook, and wash. Besides this, the sisters did her every imaginable injury— they mocked her and emptied her peas and lentils into the ashes, so that she was forced to sit and pick them out again. In the evening when she had worked till she was weary she had no bed to go to, but had to sleep by the hearth in the cinders. And as on that account she always looked dusty and dirty, they called her Cinderella.

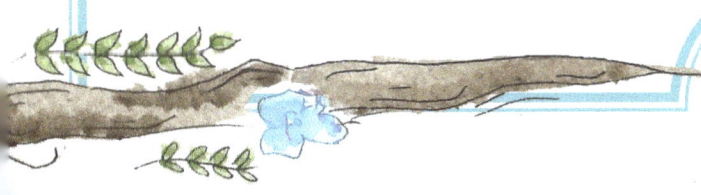

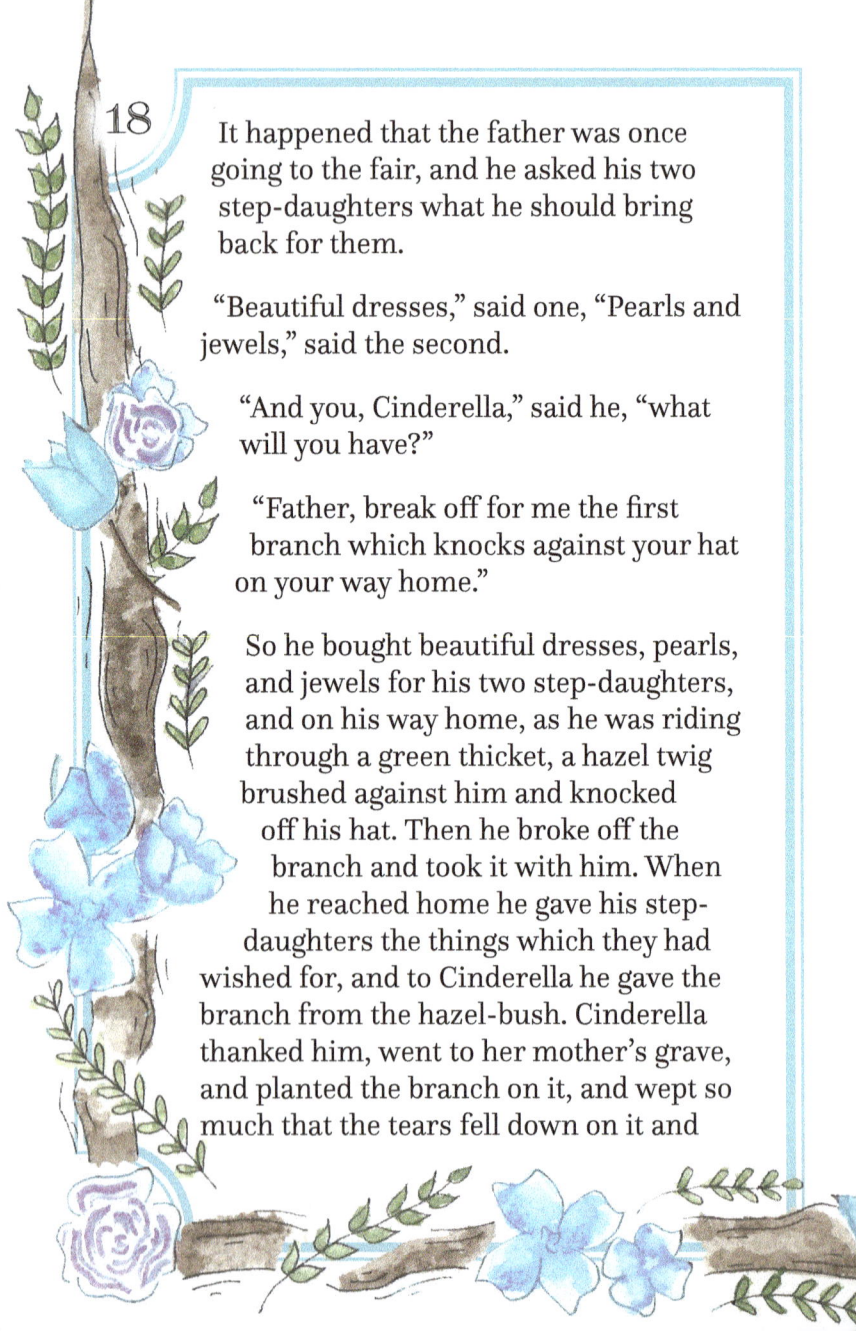

It happened that the father was once going to the fair, and he asked his two step-daughters what he should bring back for them.

"Beautiful dresses," said one, "Pearls and jewels," said the second.

"And you, Cinderella," said he, "what will you have?"

"Father, break off for me the first branch which knocks against your hat on your way home."

So he bought beautiful dresses, pearls, and jewels for his two step-daughters, and on his way home, as he was riding through a green thicket, a hazel twig brushed against him and knocked off his hat. Then he broke off the branch and took it with him. When he reached home he gave his step-daughters the things which they had wished for, and to Cinderella he gave the branch from the hazel-bush. Cinderella thanked him, went to her mother's grave, and planted the branch on it, and wept so much that the tears fell down on it and

watered it. And it grew and became a
handsome tree. Thrice a day Cinderella
went and sat beneath it, and wept and
prayed, and a little white bird always came on
the tree, and if Cinderella expressed a wish, the
bird threw down to her what she had wished for.

It happened, however, that the king gave orders
for a festival which was to last three days, and to
which all the beautiful young girls in the country
were invited, in order that his son might choose
himself a bride. When the two step-sisters heard
that they too were to appear among the number,
they were delighted, called Cinderella, and
said, "Comb our hair for us, brush our shoes,
and fasten our buckles, for we are going to the
wedding at the king's palace."

Cinderella obeyed, but wept, because she too
would have liked to go with them to the dance,
and begged her step-mother to allow her to do
so.

"You go, Cinderella," said she, "covered in dust
and dirt as you are, and would go to the festival?
You have no clothes and shoes, and yet would
dance." As, however, Cinderella went on asking,
the step-mother said at last, "I have emptied a
dish of lentils into the ashes for you, if you

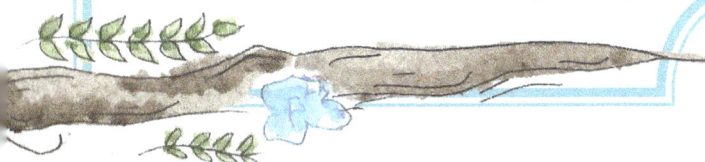
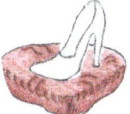

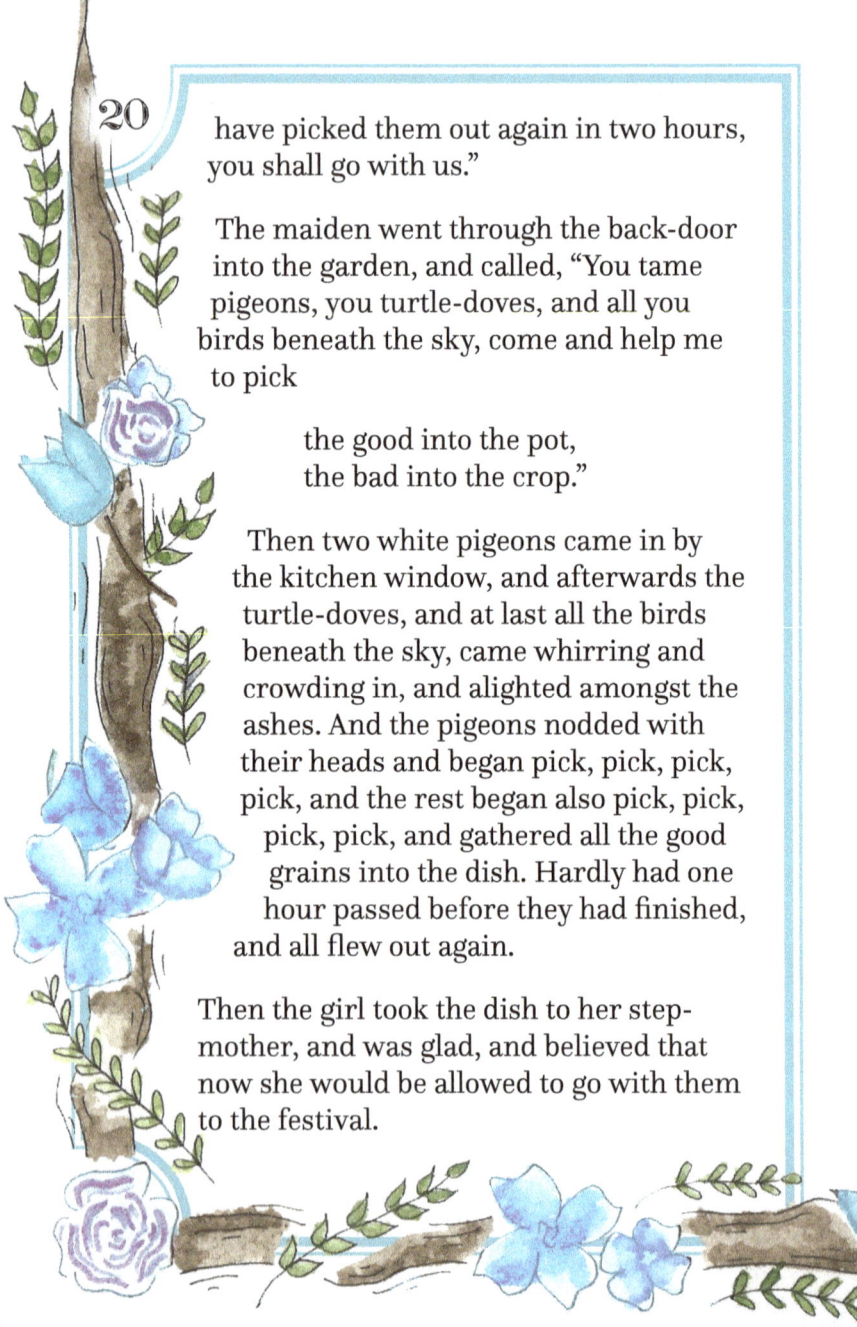

have picked them out again in two hours, you shall go with us."

The maiden went through the back-door into the garden, and called, "You tame pigeons, you turtle-doves, and all you birds beneath the sky, come and help me to pick

the good into the pot,
the bad into the crop."

Then two white pigeons came in by the kitchen window, and afterwards the turtle-doves, and at last all the birds beneath the sky, came whirring and crowding in, and alighted amongst the ashes. And the pigeons nodded with their heads and began pick, pick, pick, pick, and the rest began also pick, pick, pick, pick, and gathered all the good grains into the dish. Hardly had one hour passed before they had finished, and all flew out again.

Then the girl took the dish to her step-mother, and was glad, and believed that now she would be allowed to go with them to the festival.

But the step-mother said, "No, Cinderella, you have no clothes and you cannot dance. You would only be laughed at." And as Cinderella wept at this, the step-mother said, "If you can pick two dishes of lentils out of the ashes for me in one hour, you shall go with us." And she thought to herself, that Cinderella most certainly could not do it again.

When the step-mother had emptied the two dishes of lentils amongst the ashes, the maiden went through the back-door into the garden and cried, "You tame pigeons, you turtle-doves, and all you birds beneath the sky, come and help me to pick

> the good into the pot,
> the bad into the crop."

Then two white pigeons came in by the kitchen-window, and afterwards the turtle-doves, and at length all the birds beneath the sky, came whirring and crowding in, and alighted amongst the ashes. And the doves nodded with their heads and began pick, pick, pick, pick, and the others began also pick, pick, pick, pick, and gathered all the good seeds into the dishes, and before half an hour was over they had already finished, and all flew out again. Then the

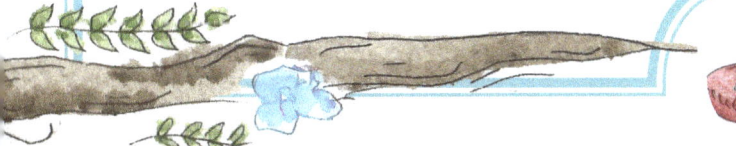

maiden was delighted, and believed that she might now go with them to the wedding.

But the step-mother said, "All this will not help. You cannot go with us, for you have no clothes and cannot dance. We should be ashamed of you." On this she turned her back on Cinderella, and hurried away with her two proud daughters.

As no one was now at home, Cinderella went to her mother's grave beneath the hazel-tree, and cried,

"Shiver and quiver, little tree, silver and gold throw down over me."

Then the bird threw a gold and silver dress down to her, and slippers embroidered with silk and silver. She put on the dress with all speed, and went to the wedding. Her step-sisters and the step-mother, however, did not know her, and thought she must be a foreign princess, for she looked so beautiful in the golden dress. They never once thought of Cinderella, and believed that she was sitting at home in the dirt, picking lentils out of the ashes. The prince approached her, took her by the hand, and danced with her. He would dance with no other maiden, and never let loose of her hand, and if any one else came to invite her, he said, "This is my partner."

She danced till it was evening, and then she wanted to go home. But the king's son said, "I will go with you and bear you company," for he wished to see to whom the beautiful maiden belonged. She escaped from him, however, and sprang into the pigeon-house. The king's son waited until her father came, and then he told him that the unknown maiden had leapt into the pigeon-house. The old man thought, "Can it be Cinderella?" And they had to bring him an axe and a pickaxe that he might hew the pigeon-house to pieces, but no one was inside it. And when they got home Cinderella lay in her dirty clothes among the ashes, and a dim little oil-lamp was burning on the mantle-piece, for Cinderella had jumped quickly down from the back of the pigeon-house and had run to the little hazel-tree, and there she had taken off her beautiful clothes and laid them on the grave, and the bird had taken them away again, and

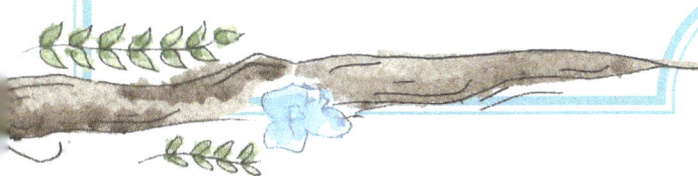

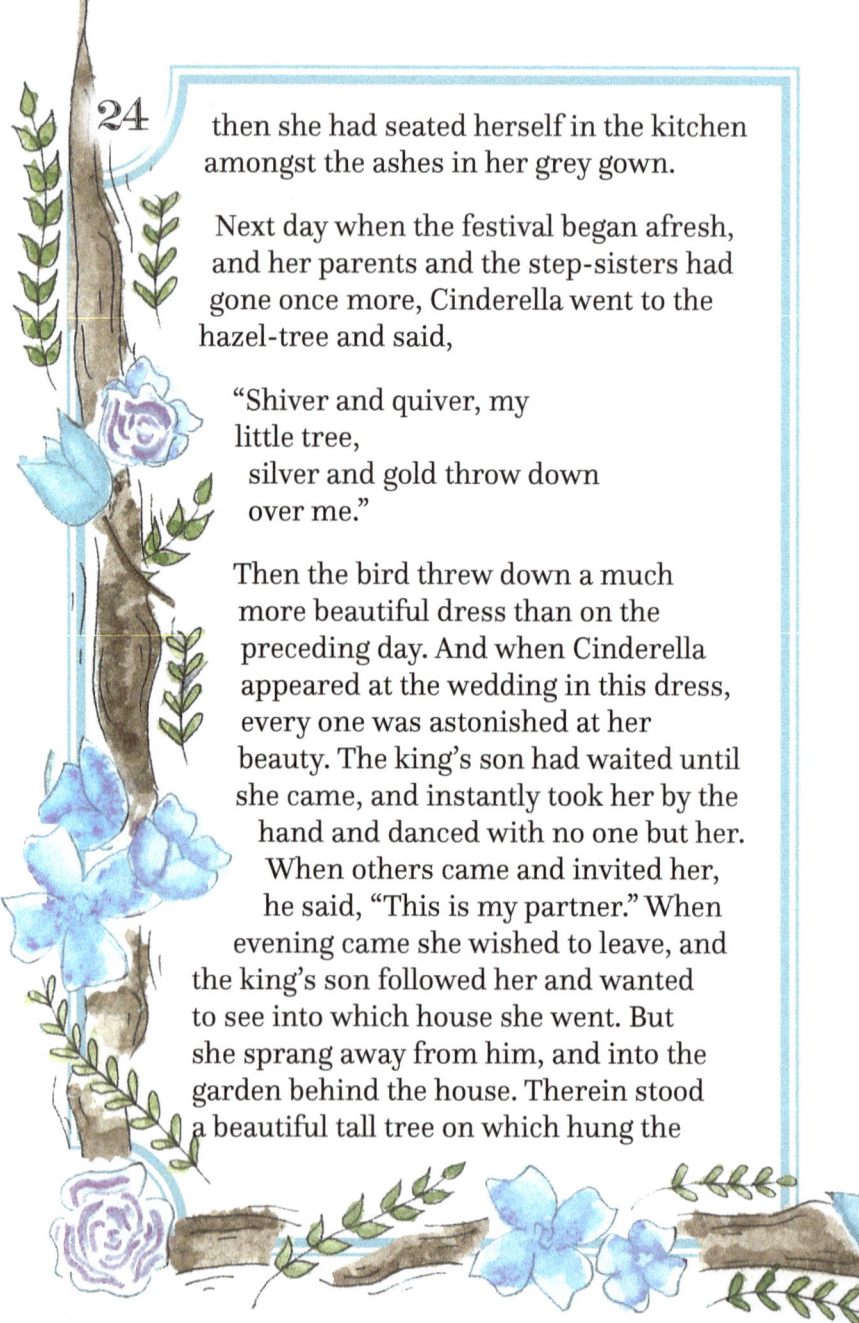

then she had seated herself in the kitchen amongst the ashes in her grey gown.

Next day when the festival began afresh, and her parents and the step-sisters had gone once more, Cinderella went to the hazel-tree and said,

"Shiver and quiver, my
little tree,
silver and gold throw down
over me."

Then the bird threw down a much more beautiful dress than on the preceding day. And when Cinderella appeared at the wedding in this dress, every one was astonished at her beauty. The king's son had waited until she came, and instantly took her by the hand and danced with no one but her. When others came and invited her, he said, "This is my partner." When evening came she wished to leave, and the king's son followed her and wanted to see into which house she went. But she sprang away from him, and into the garden behind the house. Therein stood a beautiful tall tree on which hung the

most magnificent pears. She clambered
so nimbly between the branches like a
squirrel that the king's son did not know
where she was gone. He waited until her father
came, and said to him, "The unknown maiden
has escaped from me, and I believe she has
climbed up the pear-tree." The father thought,
"Can it be Cinderella?" and had an axe brought
and cut the tree down, but no one was on it.
And when they got into the kitchen, Cinderella
lay there among the ashes, as usual, for she had
jumped down on the other side of the tree, had
taken the beautiful dress to the bird on the little
hazel-tree, and put on her grey gown.

On the third day, when the parents and sisters
had gone away, Cinderella went once more to her
mother's grave and said to the little tree,

> "Shiver and quiver, my little tree,
> silver and gold throw down over me."

And now the bird threw down to her a dress
which was more splendid and magnificent
than any she had yet had, and the slippers
were golden. And when she went to the festival
in the dress, no one knew how to speak for
astonishment. The king's son danced with her

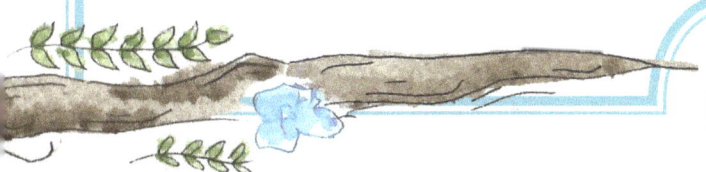

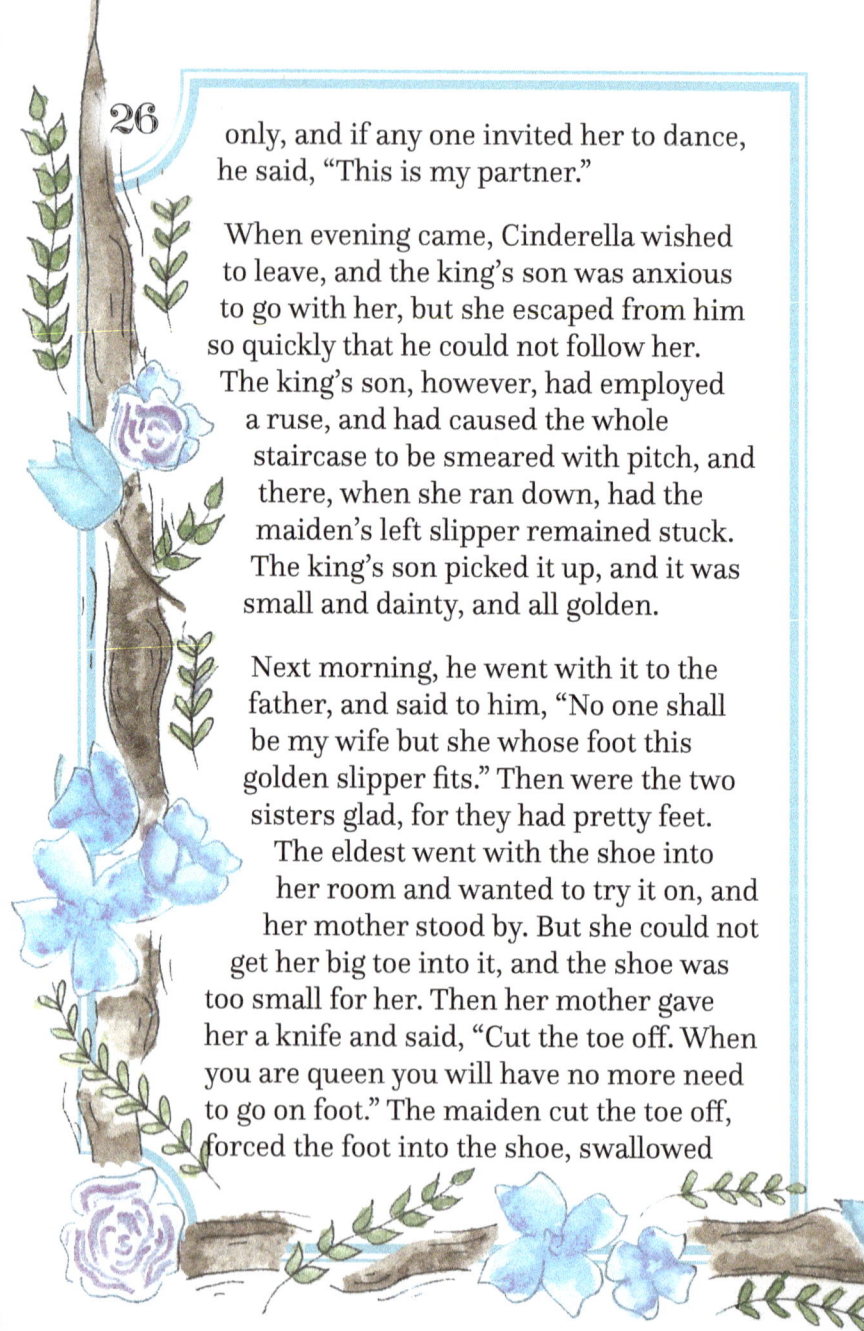

only, and if any one invited her to dance, he said, "This is my partner."

When evening came, Cinderella wished to leave, and the king's son was anxious to go with her, but she escaped from him so quickly that he could not follow her. The king's son, however, had employed a ruse, and had caused the whole staircase to be smeared with pitch, and there, when she ran down, had the maiden's left slipper remained stuck. The king's son picked it up, and it was small and dainty, and all golden.

Next morning, he went with it to the father, and said to him, "No one shall be my wife but she whose foot this golden slipper fits." Then were the two sisters glad, for they had pretty feet. The eldest went with the shoe into her room and wanted to try it on, and her mother stood by. But she could not get her big toe into it, and the shoe was too small for her. Then her mother gave her a knife and said, "Cut the toe off. When you are queen you will have no more need to go on foot." The maiden cut the toe off, forced the foot into the shoe, swallowed

the pain, and went out to the king's son.
Then he took her on his horse as his
bride and rode away with her. They were
obliged, however, to pass the grave, and there,
on the hazel-tree, sat the two pigeons and cried,

> "Turn and peep, turn and peep,
> there's blood within the shoe,
> the shoe it is too small for her,
> the true bride waits for you."

Then he looked at her foot and saw how the
blood was trickling from it. He turned his horse
round and took the false bride home again, and
said she was not the true one, and that the other
sister was to put the shoe on.

Then this one went into her chamber and got
her toes safely into the shoe, but her heel was too
large. So her mother gave her a knife and said,
"Cut a bit off your heel. When you are queen
you will have no more need to go on foot." The
maiden cut a bit off her heel, forced her foot into
the shoe, swallowed the pain, and went out to the
king's son. He took her on his horse as his bride,
and rode away with her, but when they passed
by the hazel-tree, the two pigeons sat on it and
cried,

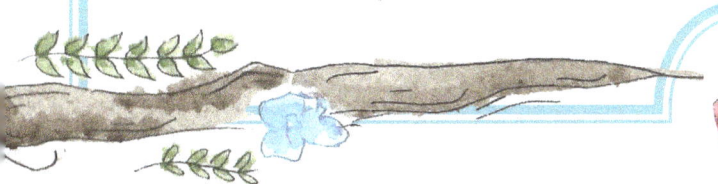

"Turn and peep, turn and peep,
there's blood within the shoe,
the shoe it is too small for her,
the true bride waits for you."

He looked down at her foot and saw how
the blood was running out of her shoe,
and how it had stained her white stocking
quite red. Then he turned his horse and
took the false bride home again. "This
also is not the right one," said he.
"Have you no other daughter?"

"No," said the man, "there is still a little
stunted kitchen-wench which my late
wife left behind her, but she cannot
possibly be the bride." The king's son
said he was to send her up to him, but
the mother answered, "Oh, no, she
is much too dirty. She cannot show
herself." But he absolutely insisted on
it, and Cinderella had to be called.

She first washed her hands and face
clean, and then went and bowed down
before the king's son, who gave her the
golden shoe. Then she seated herself on
a stool, drew her foot out of the heavy
wooden shoe, and put it into the slipper,

which fitted like a glove. And when she
rose up and the king's son looked at her
face, he recognized the beautiful maiden
who had danced with him and cried, "That is
the true bride."

The step-mother and the two sisters were
horrified and became pale with rage. He,
however, took Cinderella on his horse and rode
away with her. As they passed by the hazel-tree,
the two white doves cried,

> "Turn and peep, turn and peep,
> no blood is in the shoe,
> the shoe is not too small for her,
> the true bride rides with you."

And when they had cried that, the two came
flying down and placed themselves on
Cinderella's shoulders, one on the right, the
other on the left, and remained sitting there.

When the wedding with the king's son was to
be celebrated, the two false sisters came and
wanted to get into favor with Cinderella and
share her good fortune. When the betrothed
couple went to church, the elder was at the
right side and the younger at the left, and the
pigeons pecked out one eye from each of

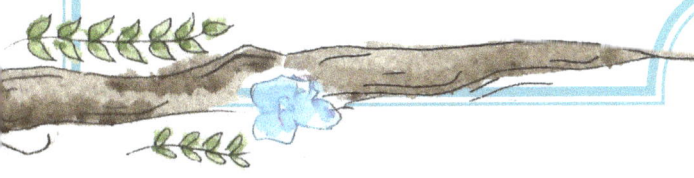

them. Afterwards as they came back the elder was at the left, and the younger at the right, and then the pigeons pecked out the other eye from each. And thus, for their wickedness and falsehood, they were punished with blindness all their days.

Translated by Margaret Hunt (1884)

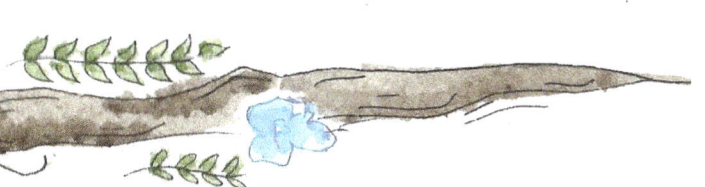

COMMENTS

Critic Bruno Bettleheim claims that, "by all accounts, 'Cinderella' is the best-known fairy tale, and probably also the best-liked" (236). He explains that it's "quite an old story...first written down in China during the ninth century A.D." though it had been an oral tale before that (236). Perrault is credited with giving "Cinderella" the "form in which it is now widely known" (236).

Every version I read of Cinderella was far more vicious than the lovely Disney version I grew up singing along to. In the one I've shared, you see how the step-mother is willing to advise her daughters to cut off pieces of their feet in hopes of becoming royalty. And the eye-pecking! Those birds are ready for some serious justice after that wedding.

In an Italian version of this story by Basile (1638), Cinderella plots with her embroidery teacher to kill her current stepmother as she wishes for the teacher to marry her father. In this case, Cinderella's neglect and harsh treatments from the teacher-turned-stepmother (who was obviously evil all along) seem deserved.

The fairy godmother; the pumpkin coach; the animals turned into horses, a driver, and footmen; the rags transformed into a beautiful gown; the glass slippers; and the call to return home before midnight (as that is when the spell shall end), which are all captured in the Disney film version, are all originally Parrault's invention (Bettleheim 261). Perhaps Disney was drawn to the humanity portrayed by Parrault's character over the Grimms' wish-granting tree. In any case, I don't see a tree singing "bibbity bobbity boop," so I suspect many would consider this a wise choice.

Hansel and Gretel

Now, little children—follow me, into
the woods. We'll build you a warm fire—stay
put this time. How you ever found your way
home last night, I'll never know. And, adieu.

Do I hear little children nibbling through
my roof? Come inside! Eat well. Rest and play!
In the morning, I'll have Hansel soufflé,
parfait, puree! And then some Gretel stew.

But you can't cook him yet, ma'am, he's too thin.
Your eyes are bad—feel his bony finger.
Your oven's too small; he couldn't fit in.
Look closely! With my shove, you will enter.

With the treasures we've found in this witch lair,
we'll go home to dad and live without care.

HANSEL & GRETEL

Jacob & Wilhelm Grimm (1812)

Hard by a great forest dwelt a poor wood-cutter with his wife and his two children. The boy was called Hansel and the girl Gretel. He had little to bite and to break, and once when great dearth fell on the land, he could no longer procure even daily bread.

Now when he thought over this by night in his bed, and tossed about in his anxiety, he groaned and said to his wife, "What is to become of us? How are we to feed our poor children, when we no longer have anything even for ourselves?"

"I'll tell you what, husband," answered the woman. "Early to-morrow morning we will take the children out into the forest to where it is the thickest. There we will light a fire for them, and give each of them one more piece of bread, and then we will go to our work and leave them alone. They will not find the way home again, and we shall be rid of them."

"No, wife," said the man, "I will not do that. How can I bear to leave my children alone in the forest? The wild animals would soon come and tear them to pieces."

"O' you fool," said she, "then we must all four die of hunger. You may as well plane the planks for our coffins," and she left him no peace until he consented.

"But I feel very sorry for the poor children, all the same," said the man. The two children had also not been able to sleep for hunger, and had heard what their step-mother had said to their father.

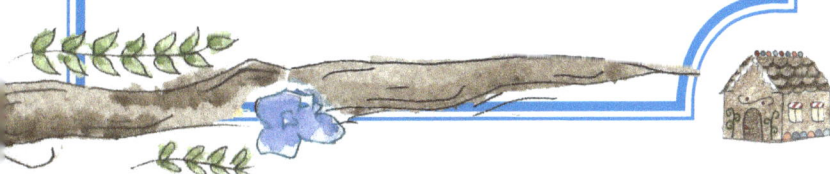

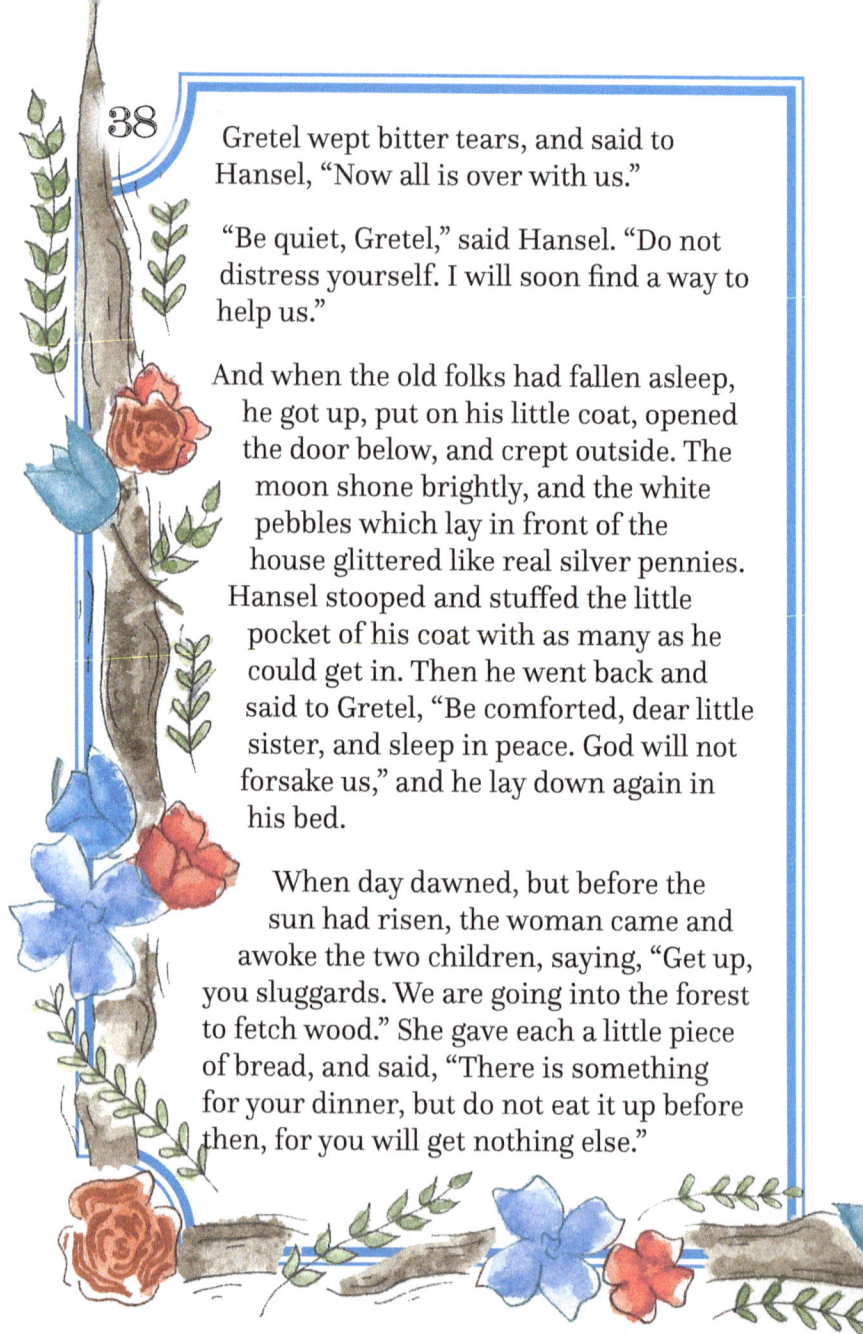

Gretel wept bitter tears, and said to Hansel, "Now all is over with us."

"Be quiet, Gretel," said Hansel. "Do not distress yourself. I will soon find a way to help us."

And when the old folks had fallen asleep, he got up, put on his little coat, opened the door below, and crept outside. The moon shone brightly, and the white pebbles which lay in front of the house glittered like real silver pennies. Hansel stooped and stuffed the little pocket of his coat with as many as he could get in. Then he went back and said to Gretel, "Be comforted, dear little sister, and sleep in peace. God will not forsake us," and he lay down again in his bed.

When day dawned, but before the sun had risen, the woman came and awoke the two children, saying, "Get up, you sluggards. We are going into the forest to fetch wood." She gave each a little piece of bread, and said, "There is something for your dinner, but do not eat it up before then, for you will get nothing else."

Gretel took the bread under her apron,
as Hansel had the pebbles in his pocket.
Then they all set out together on the way to
the forest. When they had walked a short time,
Hansel stood still and peeped back at the house,
and did so again and again.

His father said, "Hansel, what are you looking at
there and staying behind for? Pay attention, and
do not forget how to use your legs."

"Ah, father," said Hansel, "I am looking at my
little white cat, which is sitting up on the roof,
and wants to say good-bye to me."

The wife said, "Fool, that is not your little cat.
That is the morning sun which is shining on
the chimneys." Hansel, however, had not been
looking back at the cat, but had been constantly
throwing one of the white pebble-stones out of
his pocket on the road.

When they had reached the middle of the forest,
the father said, "Now, children, pile up some
wood, and I will light a fire that you may not be
cold." Hansel and Gretel gathered brushwood
together, as high as a little hill.

The brushwood was lighted, and when

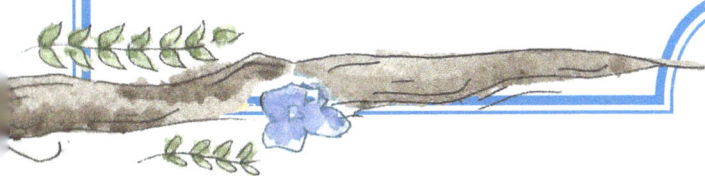

the flames were burning very high, the woman said, "Now, children, lay yourselves down by the fire and rest. We will go into the forest and cut some wood. When we have done, we will come back and fetch you away."

Hansel and Gretel sat by the fire, and when noon came, each ate a little piece of bread, and as they heard the strokes of the wood-axe, they believed that their father was near. It was not the axe, however, but a branch which he had fastened to a withered tree which the wind was blowing backwards and forwards. And as they had been sitting such a long time, their eyes closed with fatigue, and they fell fast asleep. When at last they awoke, it was already dark night.

Gretel began to cry and said, "How are we to get out of the forest now?"

But Hansel comforted her and said, "Just wait a little, until the moon has risen, and then we will soon find the way." And when the full moon had risen, Hansel took his little sister by the hand, and followed the pebbles which shone like newly-coined silver pieces, and showed them the way.

They walked the whole night long, and by break of day came once more to their father's house. They knocked at the door, and when the woman opened it and saw that it was Hansel and Gretel, she said, "You naughty children, why have you slept so long in the forest? We thought you were never coming back at all." The father, however, rejoiced, for it had cut him to the heart to leave them behind alone.

Not long afterwards, there was once more great dearth throughout the land, and the children heard their mother saying at night to their father, "Everything is eaten again, we have one half loaf left, and that is the end. The children must go. We will take them farther into the wood, so that they will not find their way out again. There is no other means of saving ourselves." The man's heart was heavy, and he thought, "It would be better for you to share the last mouthful with your children."

The woman, however, would listen to nothing that he had to say, but scolded and reproached him. He who says A must say B, likewise, and as

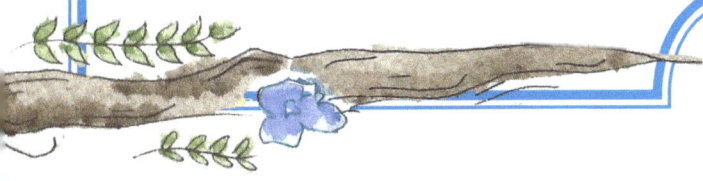

he had yielded the first time, he had to do so a second time also.

The children, however, were still awake and had heard the conversation. When the old folks were asleep, Hansel again got up, and wanted to go out and pick up pebbles as he had done before, but the woman had locked the door, and Hansel could not get out. Nevertheless he comforted his little sister, and said, "Do not cry, Gretel, go to sleep quietly, the good God will help us."

Early in the morning came the woman, and took the children out of their beds. Their piece of bread was given to them, but it was still smaller than the time before. On the way into the forest Hansel crumbled his in his pocket, and often stood still and threw a morsel on the ground. "Hansel, why do you stop and look round?" said the father. "Go on."

"I am looking back at my little pigeon which is sitting on the roof, and wants to say good-bye to me," answered Hansel.

"Fool," said the woman, "that is not your little pigeon. That is the morning sun that is shining on the chimney." Hansel, however, little by little, threw all the crumbs on the path.

The woman led the children still deeper into the forest, where they had never in their lives been before. Then a great fire was again made, and the mother said, "Just sit there, you children, and when you are tired you may sleep a little. We are going into the forest to cut wood, and in the evening when we are done, we will come and fetch you away." When it was noon, Gretel shared her piece of bread with Hansel, who had scattered his by the way. Then they fell asleep and evening passed, but no one came to the poor children.

They did not awake until it was dark night, and Hansel comforted his little sister and said, "Just wait, Gretel, until the moon rises, and then we shall see the crumbs of bread which I have strewn about. They will show us our way home again." When the moon came they set out, but they found no crumbs, for the many thousands of birds which fly about in the woods and fields had picked them all up.

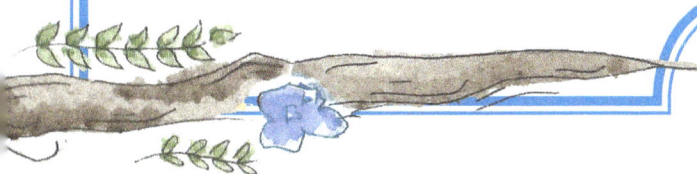

Hansel said to Gretel, "We shall soon find the way," but they did not find it. They walked the whole night and all the next day too from morning till evening, but they did not get out of the forest, and were very hungry, for they had nothing to eat but two or three berries, which grew on the ground. And as they were so weary that their legs would carry them no longer, they lay down beneath a tree and fell asleep.

It was now three mornings since they had left their father's house. They began to walk again, but they always came deeper into the forest, and if help did not come soon, they must die of hunger and weariness. When it was mid-day, they saw a beautiful snow-white bird sitting on a bough, which sang so delightfully that they stood still and listened to it. And when its song was over, it spread its wings and flew away before them, and they followed it until they reached a little house, on the roof of which it alighted. And when they approached the little house they saw that it was built of

bread and covered with cakes, but that
the windows were of clear sugar.

"We will set to work on that," said Hansel,
"and have a good meal. I will eat a bit of the roof,
and you Gretel, can eat some of the window. It
will taste sweet." Hansel reached up above, and
broke off a little of the roof to try how it tasted,
and Gretel leant against the window and nibbled
at the panes.

Then a soft voice cried from the parlor—

> "Nibble, nibble, gnaw,
> who is nibbling at my little house?"

The children answered—

> "The wind, the wind,
> the heaven-born wind,"

and went on eating without disturbing
themselves. Hansel, who liked the taste of the
roof, tore down a great piece of it, and Gretel
pushed out the whole of one round window-
pane, sat down, and enjoyed herself with it.
Suddenly the door opened, and a woman as old
as the hills, who supported herself on crutches,
came creeping out. Hansel and Gretel were so

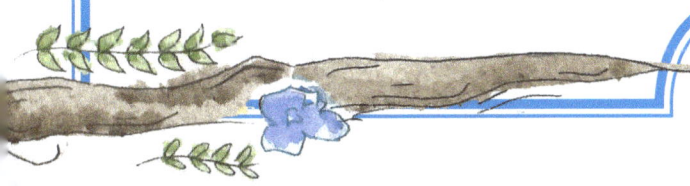

terribly frightened that they let fall what they had in their hands.

The old woman, however, nodded her head, and said, "Oh, you dear children, who has brought you here? Do come in, and stay with me. No harm shall happen to you." She took them both by the hand, and led them into her little house. Then good food was set before them, milk and pancakes, with sugar, apples, and nuts. Afterwards two pretty little beds were covered with clean white linen, and Hansel and Gretel lay down in them, and thought they were in heaven.

The old woman had only pretended to be so kind. She was in reality a wicked witch, who lay in wait for children, and had only built the little house of bread in order to entice them there. When a child fell into her power, she killed it, cooked and ate it, and that was a feast day with her. Witches have red eyes, and cannot see far, but they have a keen scent like the beasts, and are aware when human beings draw near.

When Hansel and Gretel came into her

neighborhood, she laughed with malice, and said mockingly, "I have them. They shall not escape me again."

Early in the morning before the children were awake, she was already up, and when she saw both of them sleeping and looking so pretty, with their plump and rosy cheeks, she muttered to herself, "That will be a dainty mouthful." Then she seized Hansel with her shriveled hand, carried him into a little stable, and locked him in behind a grated door. Scream as he might, it would not help him.

Then she went to Gretel, shook her till she awoke, and cried, "Get up, lazy thing, fetch some water, and cook something good for your brother. He is in the stable outside, and is to be made fat. When he is fat, I will eat him." Gretel began to weep bitterly, but it was all in vain, for she was forced to do what the wicked witch commanded.

And now the best food was cooked for poor Hansel, but Gretel got nothing but crab-shells.

Every morning the woman crept to the little stable, and cried, "Hansel, stretch out your finger that I may feel if you will soon be fat."

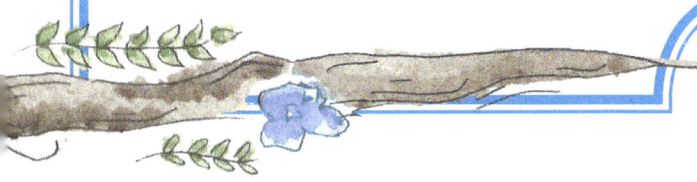

Hansel, however, stretched out a little bone to her, and the old woman, who had dim eyes, could not see it, and thought it was Hansel's finger, and was astonished that there was no way of fattening him. When four weeks had gone by, and Hansel still remained thin, she was seized with impatience and would not wait any longer.

"Now, then, Gretel," she cried to the girl, "stir yourself, and bring some water. Let Hansel be fat or lean, to-morrow I will kill him, and cook him."

Ah, how the poor little sister did lament when she had to fetch the water, and how her tears did flow down her cheeks. "Dear God, do help us," she cried. "If the wild beasts in the forest had but devoured us, we should at any rate have died together."

"Just keep your noise to yourself," said the old woman. "It won't help you at all."

Early in the morning, Gretel had to go out and hang up the cauldron with the water, and light the fire. "We will bake first," said the old woman. "I have already heated the oven, and kneaded the dough."

She pushed poor Gretel out to the oven, from which flames of fire were already darting. "Creep in," said the witch, "and see if it properly heated, so that we can put the bread in." And once Gretel was inside, she intended to shut the oven and let her bake in it, and then she would eat her, too.

But Gretel saw what she had in mind, and said, "I do not know how I am to do it. How do I get in?"

"Silly goose," said the old woman, "the door is big enough. Just look, I can get in myself," and she crept up and thrust her head into the oven. Then Gretel gave her a push that drove her far into it, and shut the iron door, and fastened the bolt. Oh. Then she began to howl quite horribly, but Gretel ran away, and the godless witch was miserably burnt to death.

Gretel, however, ran like lightning to Hansel, opened his little stable, and cried, "Hansel, we are saved. The old witch is dead."

Then Hansel sprang like a bird from its

cage when the door is opened. How they did rejoice and embrace each other, and dance about and kiss each other. And as they had no longer any need to fear her, they went into the witch's house, and in every corner there stood chests full of pearls and jewels.

"These are far better than pebbles," said Hansel, and thrust into his pockets whatever could be got in.

And Gretel said, "I, too, will take something home with me," and filled her pinafore full.

"But now we must be off," said Hansel, "that we may get out of the witch's forest."

When they had walked for two hours, they came to a great stretch of water.

"We cannot cross," said Hansel. "I see no foot-plank, and no bridge."

"And there is also no ferry," answered Gretel, "but a white duck is swimming there. If I ask her, she will help us over." Then she cried—

"Little duck, little duck,
dost thou see,
Hansel and Gretel are
waiting for thee.
There's never a plank, or bridge in sight,
take us across on thy back so white."

The duck came to them, and Hansel seated himself on its back, and told his sister to sit by him. "No," replied Gretel, "that will be too heavy for the little duck. She shall take us across, one after the other."

The good little duck did so, and when they were once safely across and had walked for a short time, the forest seemed to be more and more familiar to them, and at length they saw from afar their father's house. Then they began to run, rushed into the parlor, and threw themselves round their father's neck. The man had not known one happy hour since he had left the children in the forest. The woman, however, was dead. Gretel emptied her pinafore until pearls and precious stones ran about the room, and Hansel threw one handful after another out of his pocket to add to them. Then all anxiety was at an end, and they lived together in perfect happiness.

52

My tale is done, there runs a mouse, whosoever catches it, may make himself a big fur cap out of it.

Translated by Margaret Hunt (1884)

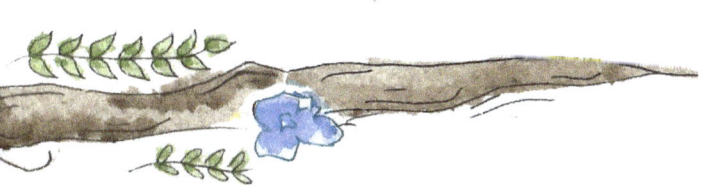

COMMENTS

My main noted variations in the versions of "Hansel and Gretel" relate to their parents. Sometimes the woman is "mother" and sometimes "step-mother." The latter seems less painful, I suppose, and also offers the popular wicked-stepmother stock character. Also, at times the father is far more willing to abandon his children than at others. If he isn't willing, the mother (or step-mother) is written as a more domineering type, pushing him to make a decision he doesn't wish to make.

Is "Hansel and Gretel" an initiation tale? As I looked into it, I found that to be likely. The story doesn't seem to point to the moral "don't eat on a stranger's house," but, instead, the lesson is to meet the challenges presented to us. After all, though the children are punished for devouring walls by being placed in danger with the risk of being eaten themselves, in the end they "live much more happily ever afterward" (Bettleheim 163). The story's warning is more so "against regression" than against gluttony or interaction with strangers; it's "an encouragement of growth toward a higher plane of psychological and intellectual existence"

(165) as seen by their crafty tricking of the witch. The two children work together to free themselves. In the end, readers can see that, using wit and unity, we can rid ourselves of great foes and solve the challenges we face.

'14 Relanne Mae

Snow White

Mirror, Mirror, Mirror: as you hang there,
tell us who in this land is most fair. Tell
us of a bewitching queen with a fear-
filled jealousy—an obsession compel-
ling her to ask: "Who?" And for a while, quell-
ing her daily dread came the answer: "You!"
Until her very-own stepdaughter well
exceeded (a thousand times) that queen's beauty. Tell us of the queen's four failed schemes, too:
of the hitman who faked Snow White's death; of
the seven who unwound tight laces, drew
out poisoned comb; and of the prince in love.
On route to his castle, her casket fell:
poisoned fruit loosed, she lived. Tell, mirror, tell!

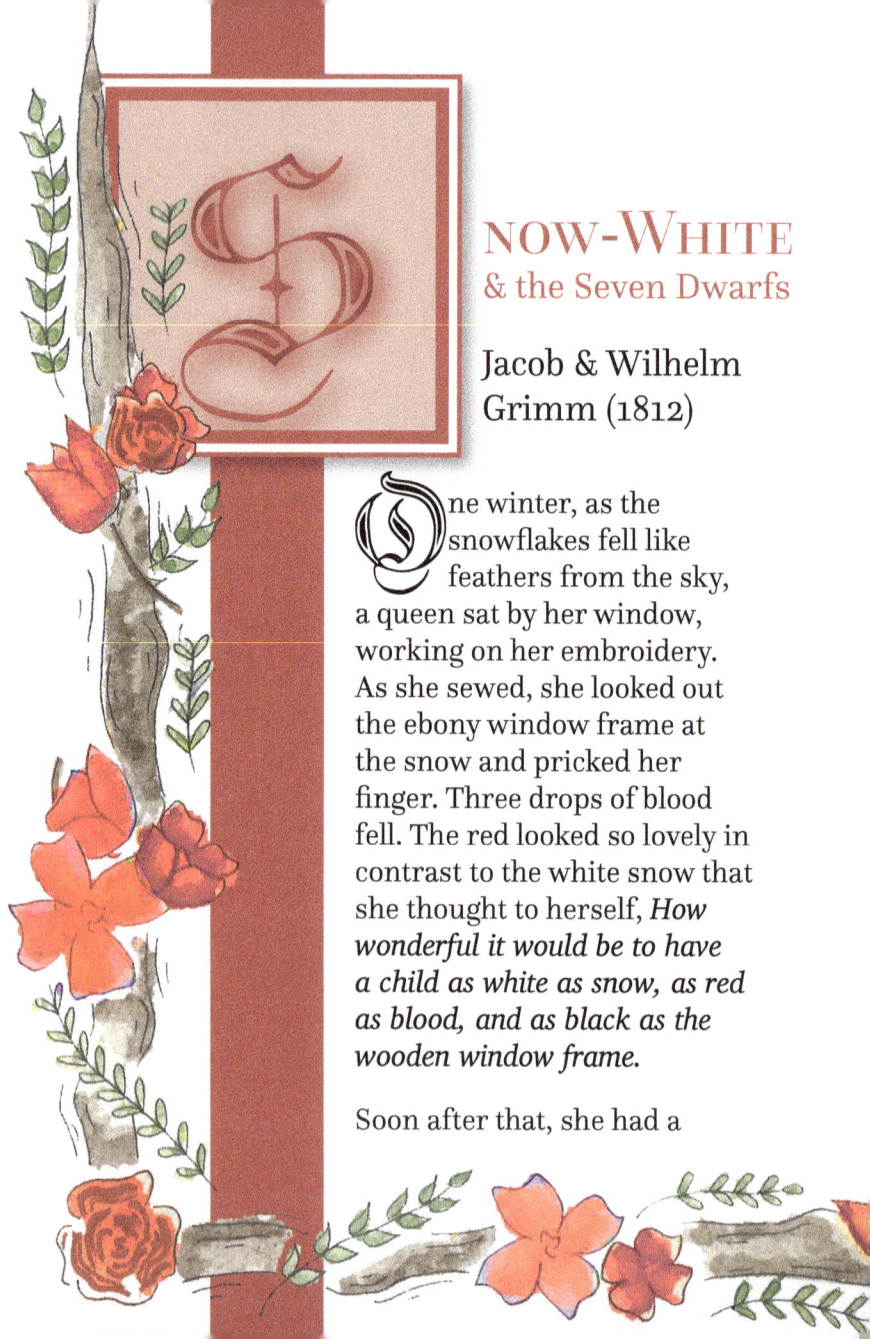

Snow-White
& the Seven Dwarfs

Jacob & Wilhelm
Grimm (1812)

One winter, as the snowflakes fell like feathers from the sky, a queen sat by her window, working on her embroidery. As she sewed, she looked out the ebony window frame at the snow and pricked her finger. Three drops of blood fell. The red looked so lovely in contrast to the white snow that she thought to herself, *How wonderful it would be to have a child as white as snow, as red as blood, and as black as the wooden window frame.*

Soon after that, she had a

daughter who was white as the snow,
with lips as red as blood and hair as black
as ebony. So they called her Snow-White.
And when the baby was born, the queen died.

A year later, the king married again. His new
wife was beautiful, but also arrogant and proud.
She couldn't stand the idea of anyone else
surpassing her beauty. She owned a magnificent
mirror, and she would stand before it, gazing at
herself and saying,

> "Mirror, mirror, on the wall,
> who's the fairest of them all?"

The mirror would answer,

> "Thou, my queen, are fairest indeed."

Knowing the mirror spoke only the truth, the
queen was contented by its answer.

But as Snow-White grew older, she also grew
more beautiful—as beautiful as the daytime and
a thousand times more beautiful than the queen.
So one day when the queen asked,

> "Mirror, mirror, on the wall,
> who's the fairest of them all?"

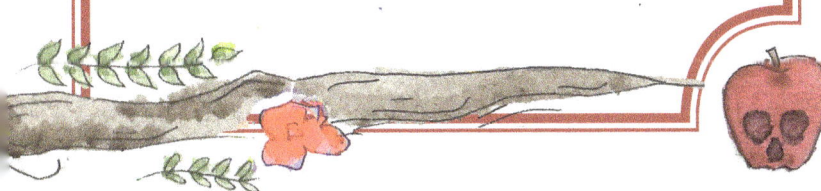

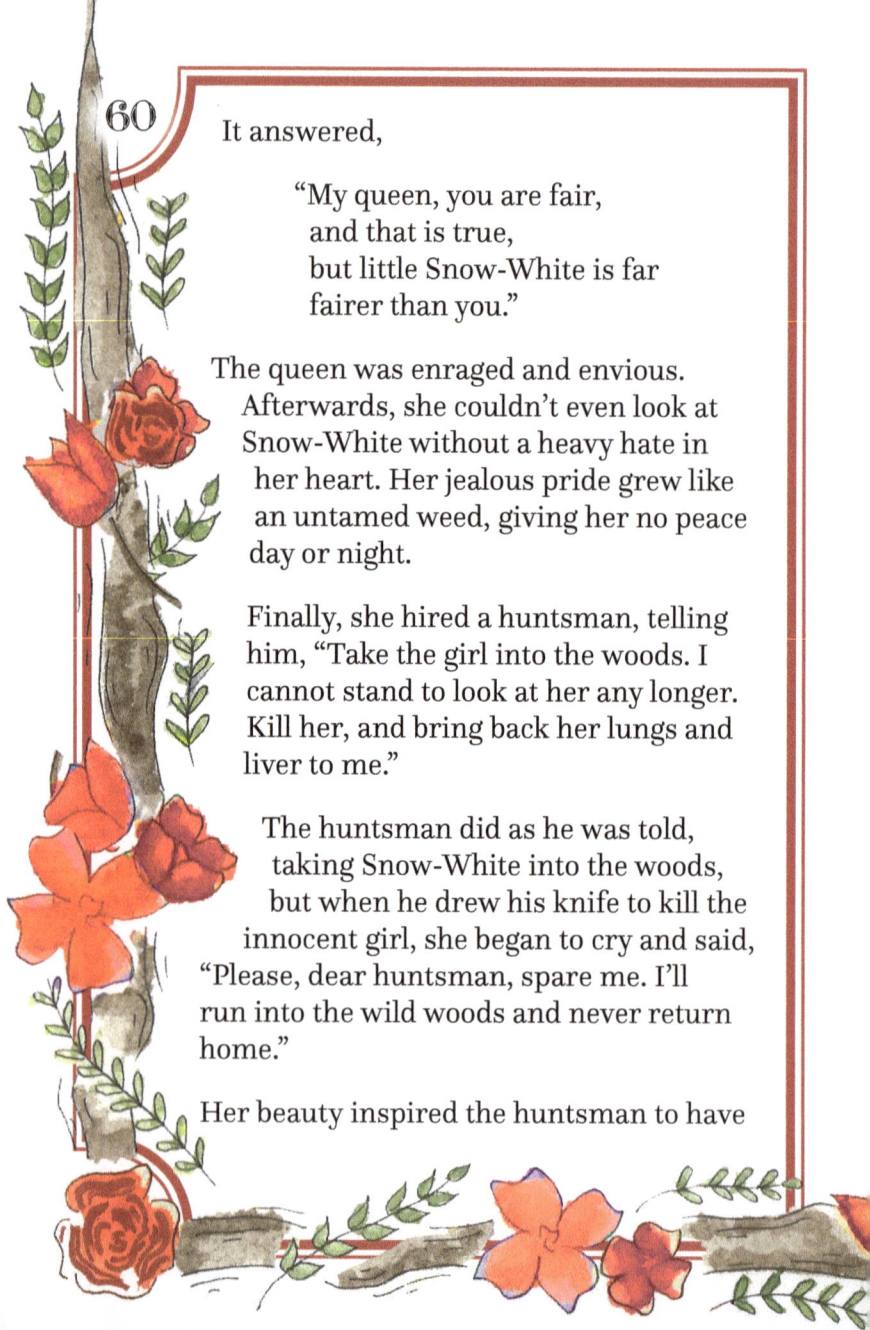

It answered,

> "My queen, you are fair,
>   and that is true,
>   but little Snow-White is far
>   fairer than you."

The queen was enraged and envious. Afterwards, she couldn't even look at Snow-White without a heavy hate in her heart. Her jealous pride grew like an untamed weed, giving her no peace day or night.

Finally, she hired a huntsman, telling him, "Take the girl into the woods. I cannot stand to look at her any longer. Kill her, and bring back her lungs and liver to me."

The huntsman did as he was told, taking Snow-White into the woods, but when he drew his knife to kill the innocent girl, she began to cry and said, "Please, dear huntsman, spare me. I'll run into the wild woods and never return home."

Her beauty inspired the huntsman to have

pity on her: "Then run away, poor child."
The beasts will eat you soon enough, he
thought, but he felt as though a weight had
been lifted from his heart because he didn't
have to be the one to kill her.

At that moment, a young bear came running by.
The huntsman killed the animal, taking its lung
and liver to the queen as proof Snow-White was
dead. The cook salted and cooked them, and the
wicked queen ate them, thinking she had eaten
the lung and liver of her rival.

Now the poor girl found herself alone in the wild
woods; she was so scared that she stared at the
fallen leaves on the ground, not knowing what
to do. Then she started to run, over rough rocks
and through thorn bushes. Though wild beasts
were all around, they did her no harm.

She ran until her legs could carry her no more.
It was almost evening, and she came upon a
little cottage. She decided to rest herself inside.
Everything in that cottage was small, neat, and
clean. On a table covered in white fabric, she
saw place settings with seven small plates; seven
small spoons, knives, and forks; and seven small
mugs. Lining a wall were seven little beds, side
by side, covered in white blankets.

Snow-White was so very hungry and thirsty that she ate a little of the vegetables and bread off of each plate and drank a drop out of each mug, because she didn't want to leave any one empty. Then she was so very tired that she lay down on each bed, one at a time, until she found the seventh one suited her. Here she said a prayer and fell asleep.

When it grew rather dark, the owners of the cottage returned home. They were seven dwarfs who worked in the mountains, digging and delving for ore. Each lit his candle, and then they could tell someone had been there.

The first said, "Who sat on my chair?"

The second, "Who ate off my plate?"

The third, "Who took some of my bread?"

The fourth, "Who ate my vegetables?"

The fifth, "Who used my fork?"

The sixth, "Who cut with my knife?"

The seventh, "Who drank out of my mug?"

Then the first looked over and said, "Who was in my bed?"

The others came over and all said, "Someone has been in my bed too!"

Except the seventh, who saw Snow-White still sleeping in his. He called the others over. They came over and looked in shock as their candles shined light on little Snow-White.

"Oh my! What a beautiful girl!" they exclaimed. They let her sleep on in the bed. The seventh dwarf slept with each of the others, one hour at a time, throughout the night.

In the morning, Snow-White woke up and was frightened at the sight of the seven dwarfs, but they were kind to her and asked her name.

"Snow-White."

They asked how she ended up at their home, and she explained about her stepmother wanting her killed, the huntsman who spared her, and the day she spent running through the wild woods until she came upon their cottage. The

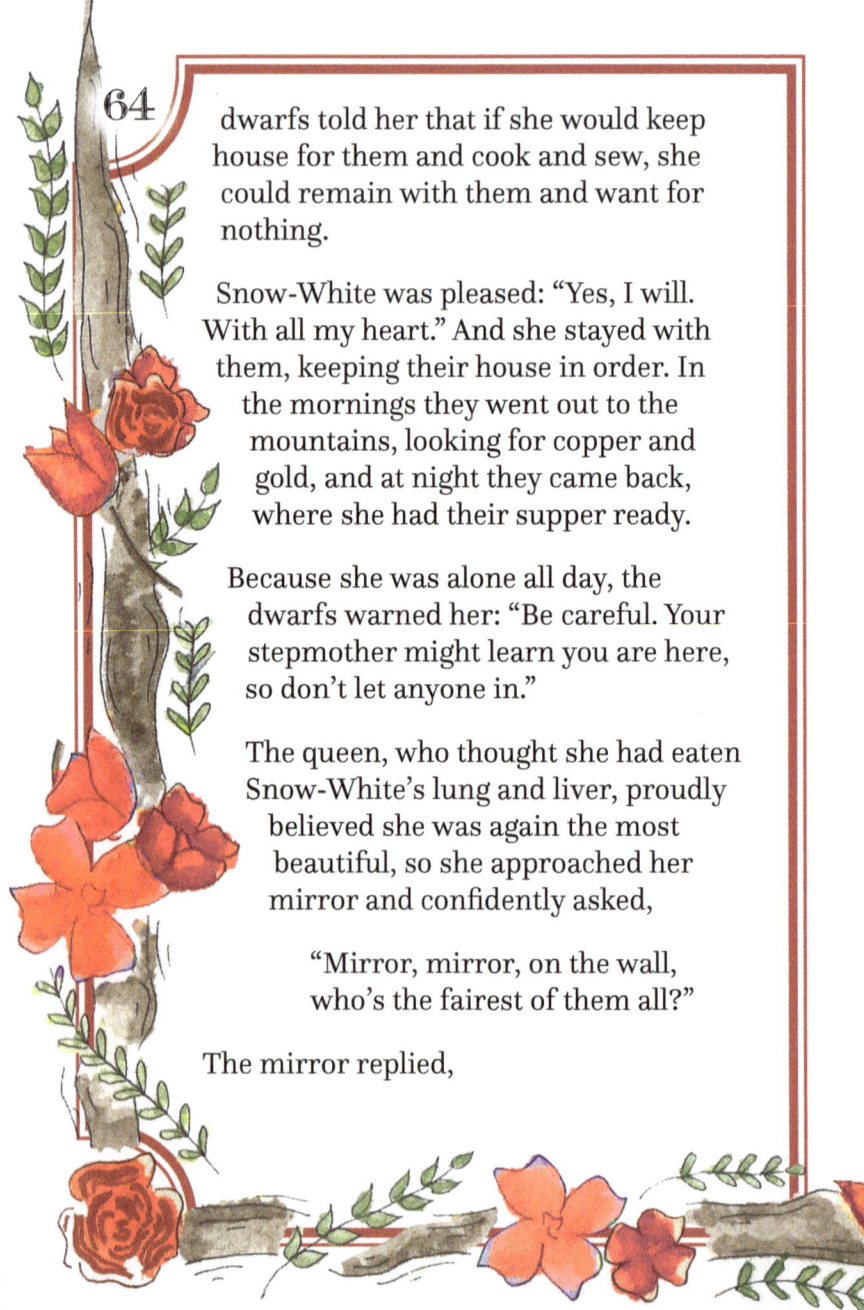

dwarfs told her that if she would keep house for them and cook and sew, she could remain with them and want for nothing.

Snow-White was pleased: "Yes, I will. With all my heart." And she stayed with them, keeping their house in order. In the mornings they went out to the mountains, looking for copper and gold, and at night they came back, where she had their supper ready.

Because she was alone all day, the dwarfs warned her: "Be careful. Your stepmother might learn you are here, so don't let anyone in."

The queen, who thought she had eaten Snow-White's lung and liver, proudly believed she was again the most beautiful, so she approached her mirror and confidently asked,

"Mirror, mirror, on the wall, who's the fairest of them all?"

The mirror replied,

"My queen, you are fair,
and that is true,
but Snow-White still is far
fairer than you—
beyond the mountains,
she found survival,
and while she breathes,
none is her rival."

The queen was surprised, but she knew the mirror never lied, that the huntsman must have, and that Snow-White was still alive. So the queen pondered intently on how she could kill Snow-White, because her pride insisted that she had to be the most beautiful in all the land. When the queen finally had an idea, she disguised herself to look like an old peddler-woman. No one would have recognized her.

Dressed thus, she went over the seven mountains to the home of the seven dwarfs, knocking on the door and calling out, "Wares for sale, cheap and pretty!"

Snow-White looked out her window and said, "Hello, good woman. What do you have for sale?"

"Good and pretty things: corsets in all colors," she replied, pulling out one made of lovely,

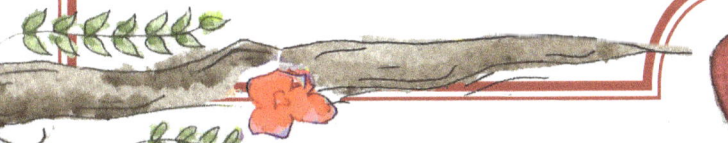

woven silk. Snow-White believed the woman to be trust-worthy and let her in. She purchased the corset and tried it on. "Child," the old woman said, "let me lace you properly." Snow-White had no misgivings and let the woman do so, but the old woman laced quickly and too tightly. Snow-White couldn't breath and fell over as if she were dead.

"You *were* the fairest," the queen said haughtily before she ran away.

Soon after the dwarfs returned home from work, shocked to see their sweet Snow-White on the ground, appearing to be dead. They picked her up and noticed she was laced up too tightly, so they cut the laces. Her breath returned, and so did her life. She explained what happened, and the dwarfs warned her, "The old peddler-woman was actually the wicked queen. Be careful, Snow-White. Don't let anyone come in when we are away."

Confident again, the queen went home and approached her mirror:

"Mirror, mirror, on the wall,
who's the fairest of them all?"

The mirror replied,

"My queen, you are fair,
and that is true,
but Snow-White still is far
fairer than you—
beyond the mountains,
she found survival,
and while she breathes,
none is her rival."

Hearing this, she felt angry and afraid, for she knew again that Snow-White was still alive. "This time, I will think of some way to truly finish you," she said, and using witchcraft this time, she made a poisoned comb and disguised herself as a different old woman. Back over the seven mountains to the home of the seven dwarfs, the queen knocked at their door and cried out, "Wares for sale, cheap and pretty."

Snow-White looked out the window and said, "Go away. I can't let anyone in."

"Well, can't you just look?" asked the woman, pulling out the poisoned comb and holding

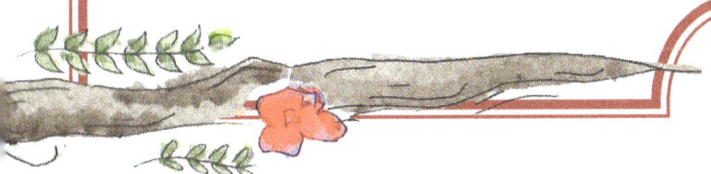

it up. Snow-White found it so pleasing that she let herself be enticed and opened up the door. When they agreed on the price, the old woman said, "Now let me properly comb your hair." Snow-White still had no misgivings and let the old woman do so, but as soon as the comb touched her hair, the poison worked its dark magic, and the girl fell over senseless.

"You quintessential beauty, now you are truly dead," said the wicked queen before she ran away.

Luckily it was again close to time for the seven dwarfs to return home, and when they did so, they saw Snow-White once again lying on the ground as if dead. They supposed it was the stepmother and found the poisoned comb. As soon as they removed it, Snow-White came to and told them what had happened. Again they warned her to be careful and open the door to no one.

At home, the queen approached her mirror:

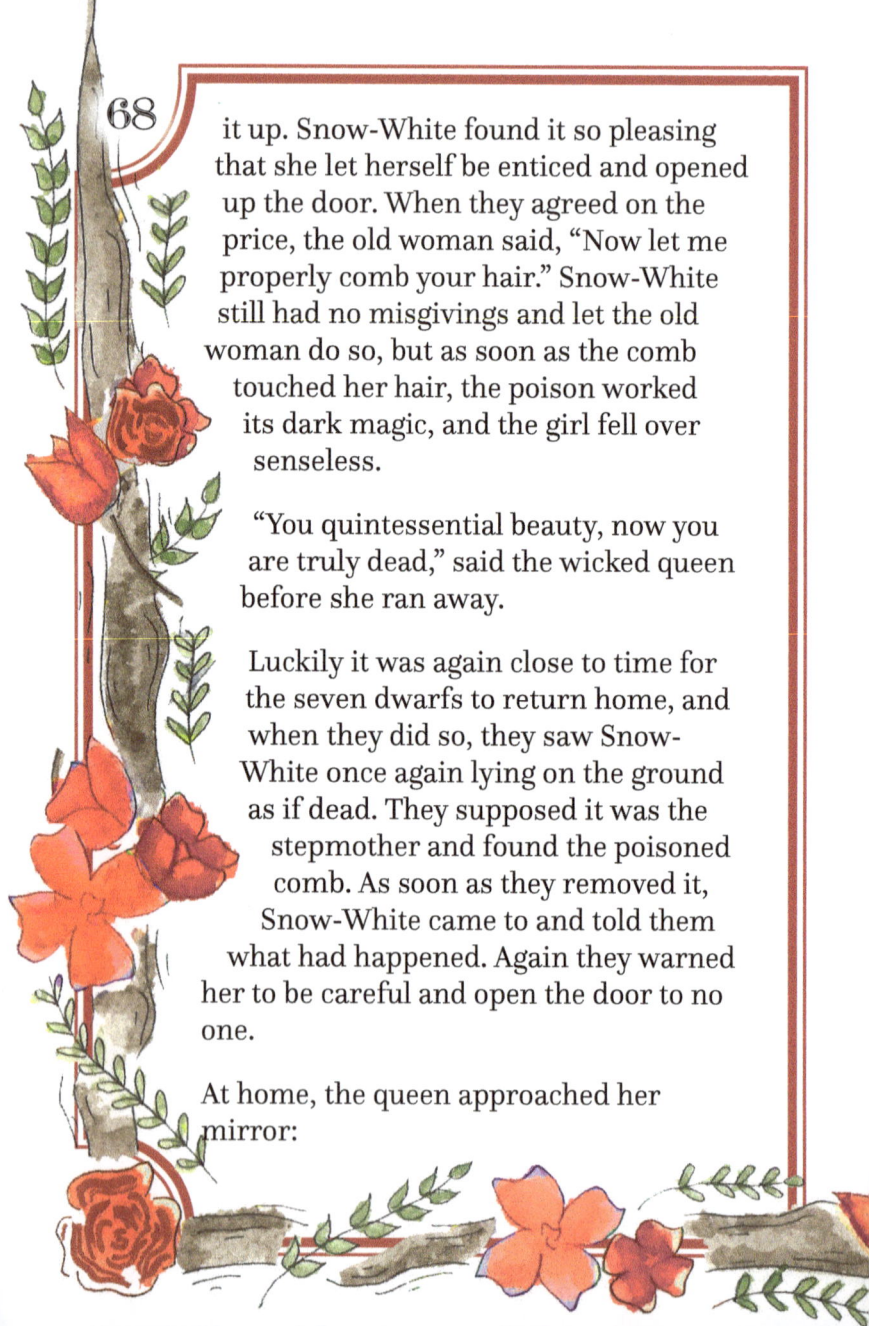

"Mirror, mirror, on the wall,
who's the fairest of them all?"

The mirror replied,

"My queen, you are fair,
and that is true,
but Snow-White still is far
fairer than you—
beyond the mountains,
she found survival,
and while she breathes,
none is her rival."

Hearing these words, she shuddered with wrath. "If it costs me my own life, Snow-White will die." With these words, she went into a private room, visited by no one, and there she made a poisoned apple. The outside looked lovely, white with a red cheek, so anyone who saw it would ache for it, but anyone who ate it would die. With her apple prepared, she disguised herself as a farmer's wife and went over the mountains to the home of the seven dwarfs. Knocking on the door, she saw Snow-White's head pop out of the window and heard her say, "The seven dwarfs have absolutely forbidden me to let anyone in."

"That's fine with me," the woman replied.

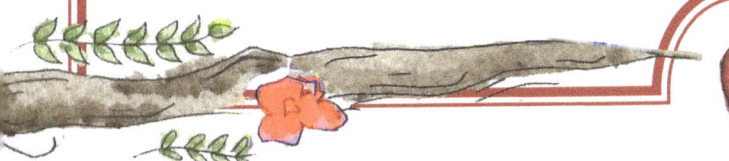

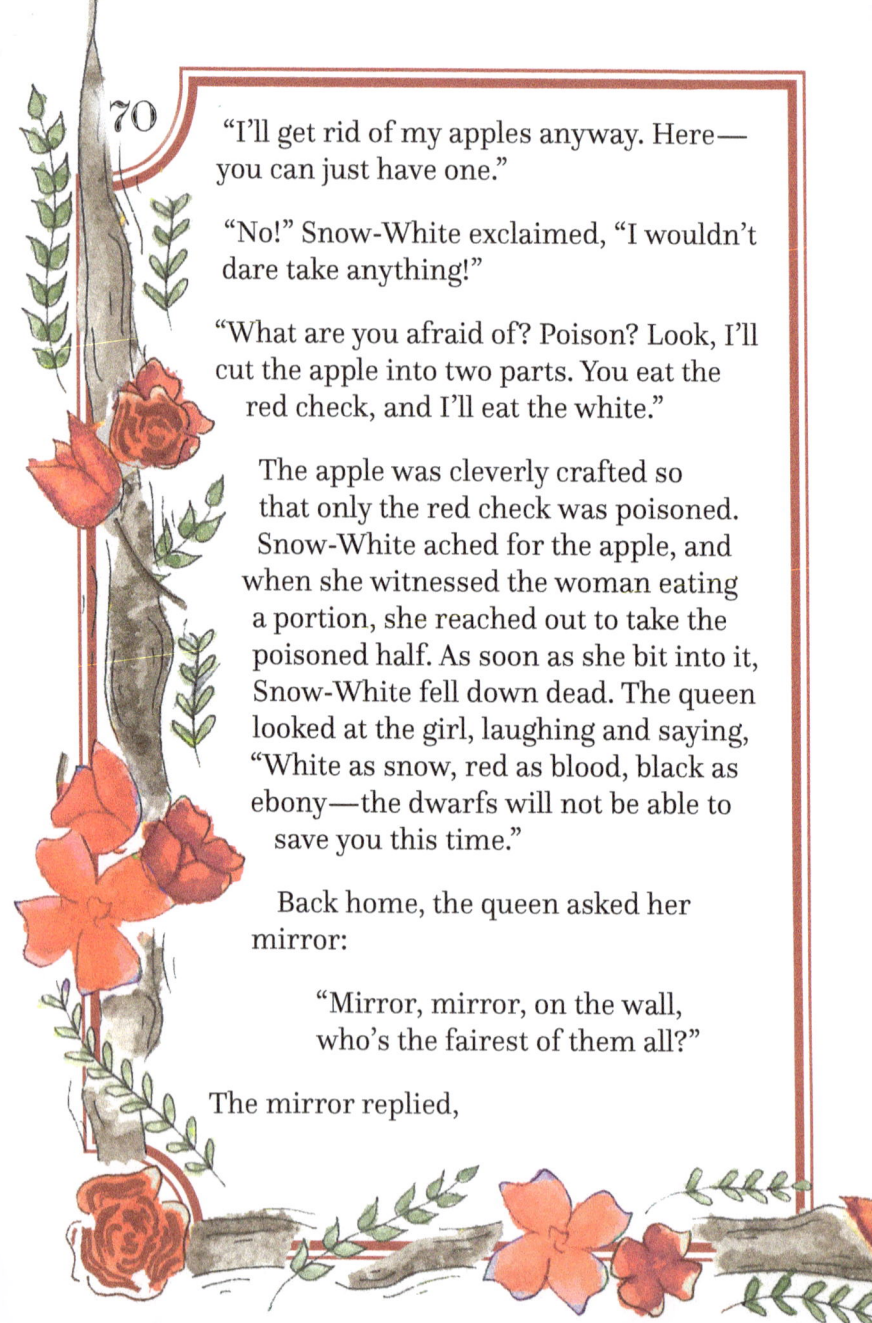

"I'll get rid of my apples anyway. Here—you can just have one."

"No!" Snow-White exclaimed, "I wouldn't dare take anything!"

"What are you afraid of? Poison? Look, I'll cut the apple into two parts. You eat the red check, and I'll eat the white."

The apple was cleverly crafted so that only the red check was poisoned. Snow-White ached for the apple, and when she witnessed the woman eating a portion, she reached out to take the poisoned half. As soon as she bit into it, Snow-White fell down dead. The queen looked at the girl, laughing and saying, "White as snow, red as blood, black as ebony—the dwarfs will not be able to save you this time."

Back home, the queen asked her mirror:

"Mirror, mirror, on the wall,
who's the fairest of them all?"

The mirror replied,

"Thou, my queen, are fairest indeed."

Her jealous and hateful heart found peace, as well as a jealous and hateful heart can.

When the seven dwarfs returned home, they found Snow-White lying on the ground, no longer breathing. They picked her up to see if they could find any poisoned object, unlaced her, combed her hair, and washed her, but nothing worked. The poor girl was dead, and dead she remained. Laying her body on a pedestal, all seven sat at her side and wept three long days. They knew they should bury her, but she still looked as if she were alive, with her beautiful red cheeks.

"We cannot bury her in the deep, dark earth," they said. So they had a glass coffin made so that her beauty could still be seen, and they laid her in it, writing her name and title in gold letters. Placing the coffin out upon the mountain, each took a turn staying by it. The birds came as well, weeping for Snow-White: first an owl, then a black raven, and finally a dove.

So Snow-White remained for quite a long time in that coffin, though she never changed and

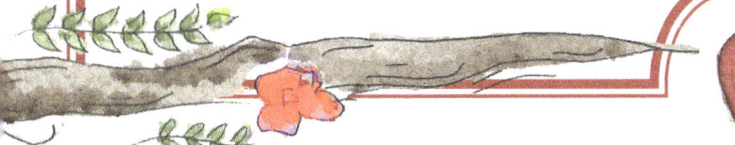

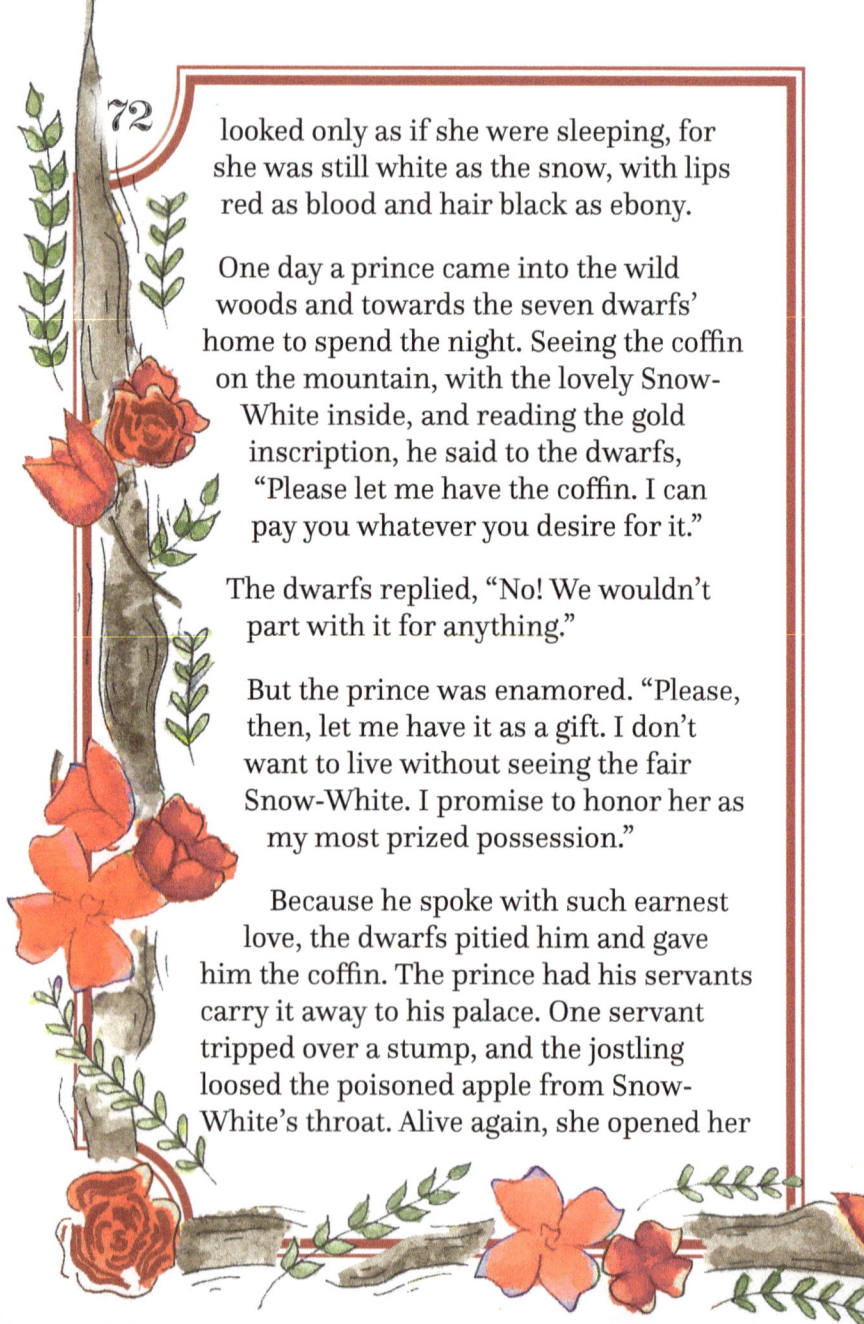

looked only as if she were sleeping, for she was still white as the snow, with lips red as blood and hair black as ebony.

One day a prince came into the wild woods and towards the seven dwarfs' home to spend the night. Seeing the coffin on the mountain, with the lovely Snow-White inside, and reading the gold inscription, he said to the dwarfs, "Please let me have the coffin. I can pay you whatever you desire for it."

The dwarfs replied, "No! We wouldn't part with it for anything."

But the prince was enamored. "Please, then, let me have it as a gift. I don't want to live without seeing the fair Snow-White. I promise to honor her as my most prized possession."

Because he spoke with such earnest love, the dwarfs pitied him and gave him the coffin. The prince had his servants carry it away to his palace. One servant tripped over a stump, and the jostling loosed the poisoned apple from Snow-White's throat. Alive again, she opened her eyes, lifted the lid of the coffin, and sat up asking, "Where am I?"

The prince was shocked but overjoyed and said, "With me!" He explained what had happened and promised her, "I love you more dearly than anything in the world. Please come with me to my father's palace and be my wife."

Snow-White agreed and went with him. They planned an extravagant wedding, inviting people from all the lands, including Snow-White's wicked stepmother. When she dressed in her finest and approached her mirror, the evil queen asked her usual question,

> "Mirror, mirror, on the wall,
> who's the fairest of them all?"

The mirror replied,

> "My queen, you are fair, and that is true,
> but the young queen is far, far
> fairer than you."

The evil woman cursed wretchedly and felt so miserable that she didn't know what to do. She didn't want to attend the wedding at all, but she finally knew she had to: she had to see the young queen, her new rival.

At the wedding, the wicked woman recognized Snow-White and froze with fear and anger. But she was caught and punished for her sins. Iron shoes were heated on the fire for her, and she was forced to wear them and dance until she fell down dead.

Rendition by Jessa R. Sexton (2016)

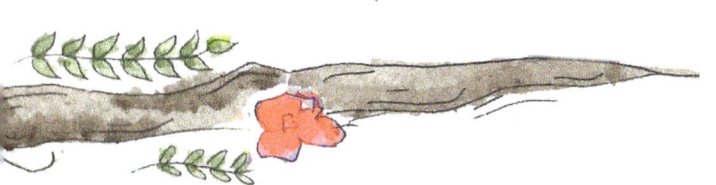

COMMENTS

The most disturbing difference I noted between an earlier version and this more popular Grimm's version of this tale is that the earlier makes Snow-White's own mother so very envious of her own daughter that she sends Snow-White out to be killed (Bettleheim 201). The authors noted this to be a little too harsh for a normal reader's consumption and changed it to a stepmother, presenting once again that evil-stepmother stock character.

Bruno Bettleheim brings up an interesting point connected to this story and "Little Red Riding Hood." Both stories introduce a life-saving hunter. Bettleheim explains, "In the unconscious the hunter is seen as the symbol of protection... the hunter of fairy tales is not a figure who kills friendly creatures, but one who dominates, controls, and subdues wild, ferocious beasts" (205). This point is even further developed in the film version *Snow White and the Huntsman*, which makes the man sent to kill the title character a title character himself instead of the passing mention in the Grimm version.

Before reading the Grimm version, I

didn't know of the multiple attempts on Snow-White's life. I suppose I have to question our heroine's intelligence (or is she just considered to be so pure that she is far too trusting?) in letting an old woman fool her three times—no matter the enchanted costume or varying story that came along with her. If only the evil queen had asked her mirror whom was the cleverest of them all, there wouldn't have been any sort of competition there. Our sweet Snow-White is lucky she's so beautiful. She captures the hearts of many, even after her death, with her beauty. And her beauty, though it is the literal death of her, is also what saves her. That and the footfall of a clumsy servant.

Rehanna Mae '16

Pyramus and Thisbe

Through a crack in the wall twixt two homes in
Babylon sweet somethings were whispered by
Pyramus and Thisbe, whose love had been
confined to covert conversations. Why?

Because, quite simply, with enmity their
parents were enemies. Yet despite that
familial ill will, these two prepared
to elope. But when Thisbe arrived at
their meeting spot, a series of quite unfortunate events occurred, causing each
to assume the other was dead. Undone
by their grief, they ended their lives. We reach
the point in this tale where we must question
why we feed our sad romance obsession.

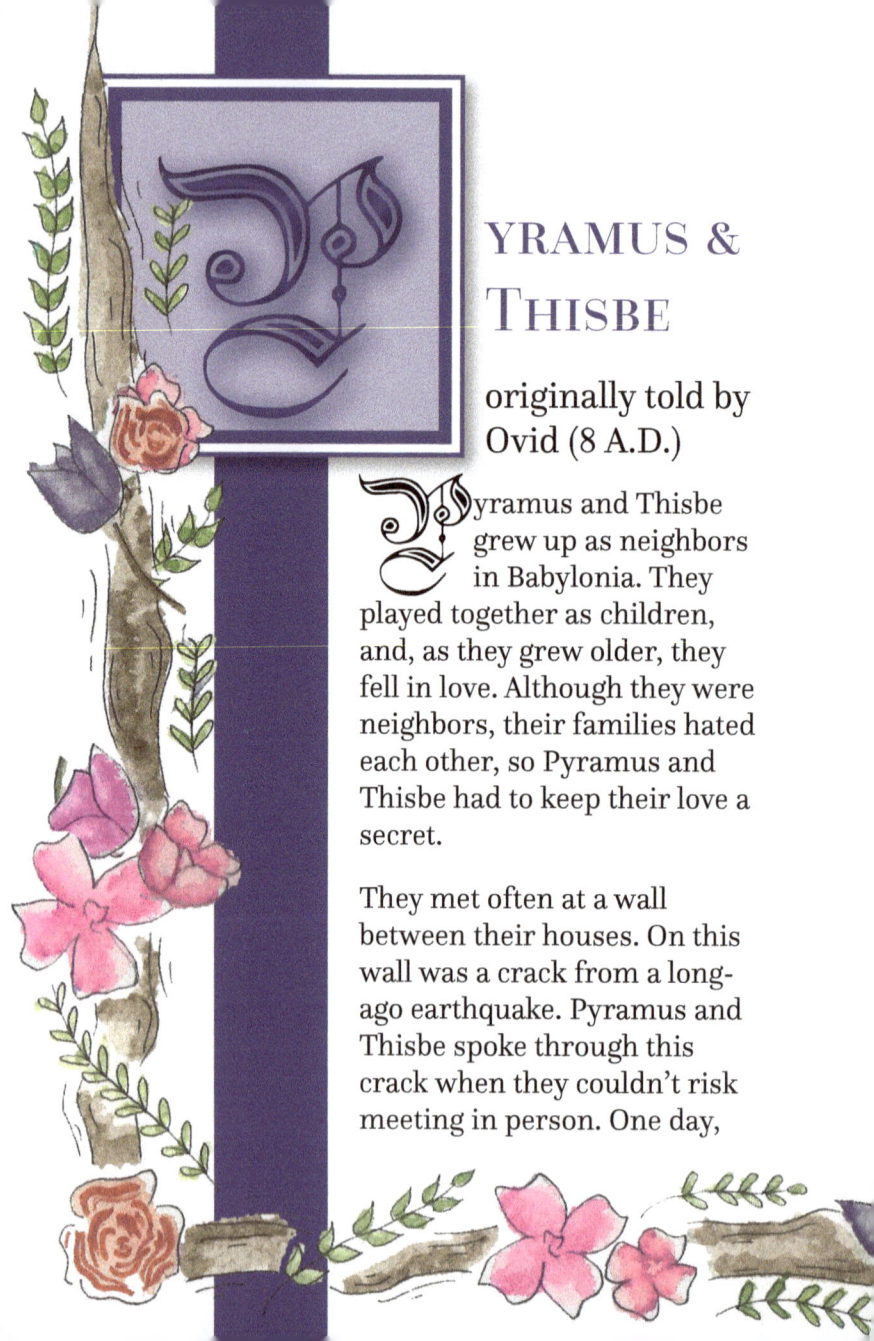

PYRAMUS & THISBE

originally told by Ovid (8 A.D.)

yramus and Thisbe grew up as neighbors in Babylonia. They played together as children, and, as they grew older, they fell in love. Although they were neighbors, their families hated each other, so Pyramus and Thisbe had to keep their love a secret.

They met often at a wall between their houses. On this wall was a crack from a long-ago earthquake. Pyramus and Thisbe spoke through this crack when they couldn't risk meeting in person. One day, the beautiful weather brought them great sadness over their situation. They cried as they saw the freedom of two hummingbirds, who were able to fly together over the wall. Immediately, they decided they wouldn't be kept apart any longer. They would meet that very night outside the city gate under the mulberry tree covered in white fruit, which grew near a stream by the graveyard.

Covered by a veil, Thisbe arrived first and waiting for Pyramus. Suddenly a lioness, jaws covered in blood from her fresh dinner, appeared and strode to the stream for a drink. Thisbe was frightened and ran to a cave, dropping her veil by accident. The lioness saw the veil, grabbed it, and shredded it—covering it in blood before striding away.

When Pyramus arrived, he noticed large paw prints. His heart raced as he approached the stream and saw Thisbe's veil torn and covered in blood. Unable to find her, Pyramus assumed she was dead and couldn't control his sorrow. He drew his sword and drove it into his side. When he removed the sword, his blood sprayed the white berries of the tree, changing them to a deep purple hue.

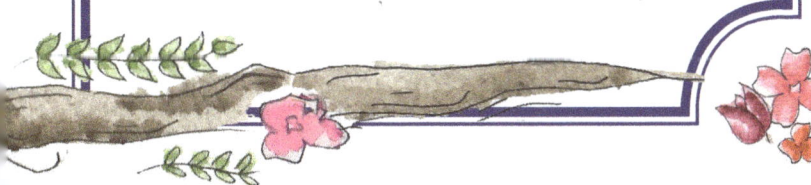

When Thisbe got over her fear, she returned to the stream and saw Pyramus's lifeless body on the ground. Overcome by uncontrollable agony, she grabbed his sword and threw herself onto it. As she lay dying, she prayed to the gods that their bodies would be buried together in one tomb and that the tree, stained by her dearest's blood, would always bear fruit this color as a reminder of their love. Even today, the berries of the mulberry tree turn a deep purple when ripe.

Rendition by Jessa R. Sexton (2016)

COMMENTS

You caught me: "Pyramus and Thisbe" is not a fairy tale. Yet I chose it for this project for a couple reasons.

1) Much like fairy tales, this is a story that has been passed down and altered throughout time. The most famous of these alterations is by Shakespeare, who sets his version in the heat of summer in Italy (because any feud is always made worse when it's horridly hot outside) and shows his audience multiple characters on each side of these warring families in one of the most famous plays of all time, *Romeo and Juliet*.

2) "Pyramus and Thisbe" follows the line of tragedy that many fairy tales hold (which are often edited out in the family-friendly kid versions and films of today). If fairy tales are supposed to teach us a lesson, what better lessons can be learned than from "uncontrollable agony," if not of your own, than of a character in a story? Is the lesson here to obey your parents? Is it that we will lose something important to us if we don't allow love to reign over hostility? (That's where Shakespeare took the tale.) If nothing else, we see that no good can come

from holding tight to bitter feuds.

3) I have loved this story since first reading it in Mrs. Napier's 9th grade English class, and, since this is my book, I included it.

'16 Rehanna Mae

Little Red Riding Hood

Come here, Little Red, always covered by
warm velvet, take this cake to your Gram's home
now—you two sweets will lift her spirit. I
warn you, dear one: stay the path. Do. Not. Roam.

Come here, Little Red—tell me where you're going. To see your Gram? Hmmm. You should pick her
flowers! Far from the path, many kinds grow.
(While you're gone, I'll make a tasty transfer.)

Come here, Little Red—what big hands I have,
ay? Well, let me show you how they'll hug you—
Big teeth? They make eating easy. I've had
one snack so far, and you'll be number two.

Come here, Little Red—climb out; the beast's dead.
Be careful whom you trust and where you're led.

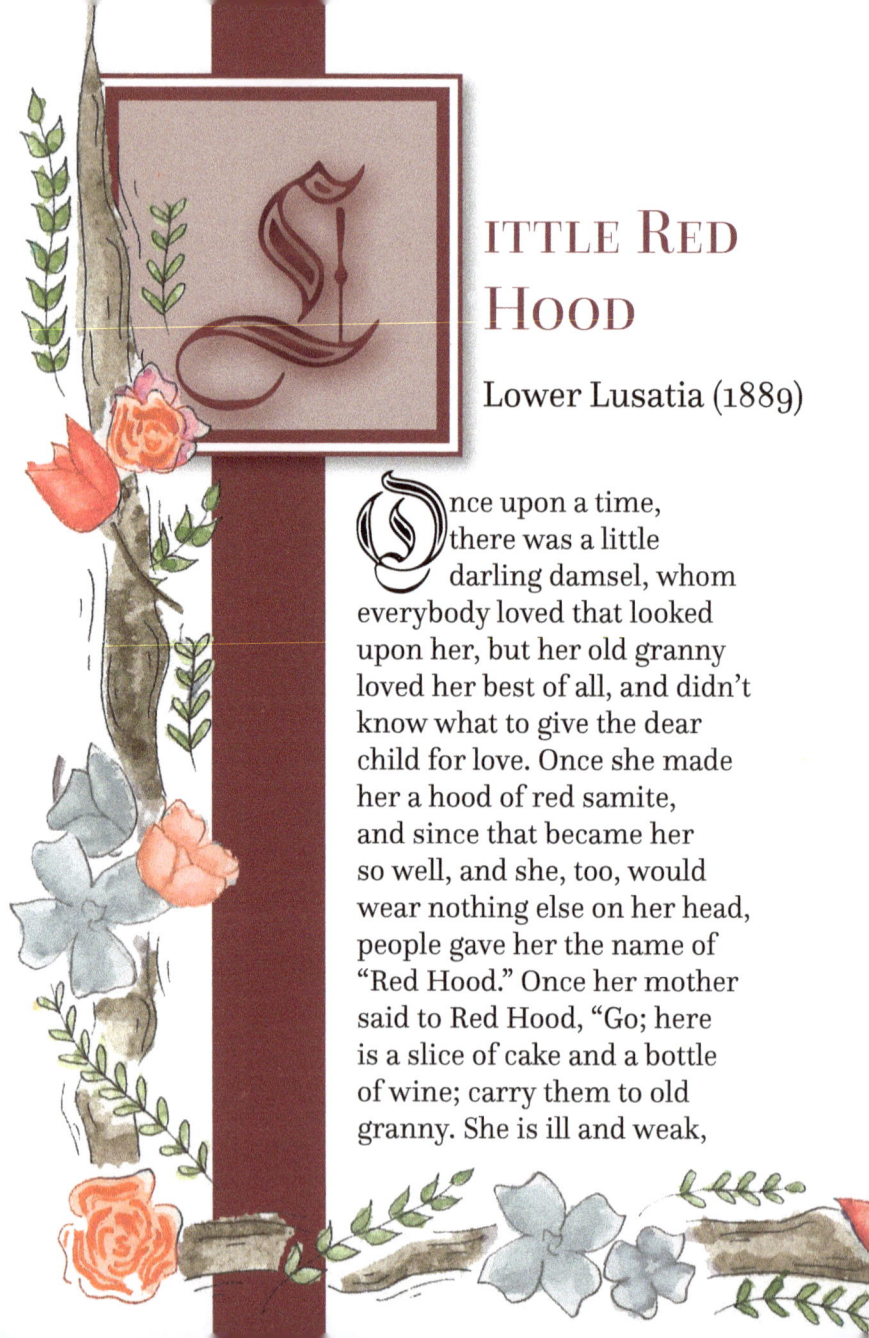

LITTLE RED HOOD

Lower Lusatia (1889)

Once upon a time, there was a little darling damsel, whom everybody loved that looked upon her, but her old granny loved her best of all, and didn't know what to give the dear child for love. Once she made her a hood of red samite, and since that became her so well, and she, too, would wear nothing else on her head, people gave her the name of "Red Hood." Once her mother said to Red Hood, "Go; here is a slice of cake and a bottle of wine; carry them to old granny. She is ill and weak, and they will refresh her. But be pretty behaved, and don't peep about in all corners when you come into her room, and don't forget to say 'Good-day.' Walk, too, prettily, and don't go out of the road, otherwise you will fall and break the bottle, and then poor granny will have nothing." Red Hood said, "I will observe everything well that you have told me," and gave her mother her hand upon it.

But granny lived out in a forest, half an hour's walk from the village. When Red Hood went into the forest, she met a wolf. But she did not know what a wicked beast he was, and was not afraid of him.

"God help you, Red Hood!" said he.

"God bless you, wolf!" replied she.

"Whither so early, Red Hood?"

"To granny."

"What have you there under your mantle?"

"Cake and wine. We baked yesterday; old granny must have a good meal for once, and strengthen herself therewith."

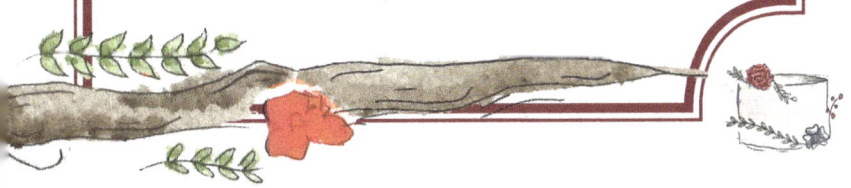

"Where does your granny live, Red Hood?"

"A good quarter of an hour's walk further in the forest, under yon three large oaks. There stands her house; further beneath are the nut-trees, which you will see there," said Red Hood.

The wolf thought within himself, "This nice young damsel is a rich morsel. She will taste better than the old woman; but you must trick her cleverly, that you may catch both."

For a time he went by Red Hood's side. Then said he, "Red Hood! Just look! There are such pretty flowers here! Why don't you look round at them all? Methinks you don't even hear how delightfully the birds are singing! You are as dull as if you were going to school, and yet it is so cheerful in the forest!"

Little Red Hood lifted up her eyes, and when she saw how the sun's rays glistened through the tops of the trees, and every place was full of flowers, she bethought herself, "If I bring with me a sweet smelling nosegay to granny, it will cheer her. It is still so early, that I shall come to her in plenty of time," and therewith she skipped into the forest and looked for flowers. And when she had plucked one, she fancied that another further off was nicer, and ran there, and went always deeper and deeper into the forest.

But the wolf went by the straight road to old granny's, and knocked at the door.

"Who's there?"

"Little Red Hood, who has brought cake and wine. Open!"

"Only press the latch," cried granny; "I am so weak that I cannot stand."

The wolf pressed the latch, walked in, and went without saying a word straight to granny's bed and ate her up. Then he took her clothes, dressed himself in them, put her cap on his head, lay down in her bed and drew the curtains.

Meanwhile little Red Hood was running after flowers, and when she had so many that she could not carry any more, she bethought her of her granny, and started on the way to her.

It seemed strange to her that the door was wide open, and when she entered the room everything seemed to her so peculiar, that she thought, "Ah! My! How strange I feel to-day, and yet at other times I am so glad to be with granny!"

She said, "Good-day!" but received no answer.

Thereupon she went to the bed and undrew the curtains. There lay granny, with her cap drawn down to her eyes, and looking so queer!

"Ah, granny! Why have you such long ears?"

"The better to hear you."

"Ah, granny! Why have you such large eyes?"

"The better to see you."

"Ah, granny! Why have you such large hands?"

"The better to take hold of you."

"But, granny! Why have you such a terribly large mouth?"

"The better to eat you up!"

And therewith the wolf sprang out of bed at once on poor little Red Hood, and ate her up. When the wolf had satisfied his appetite, he lay down again in the bed, and began to snore tremendously.

A huntsman came past, and bethought himself, "How can an old woman snore like that? I'll just have a look to see what it is."

He went into the room, and looked into the bed; there lay the wolf. "Have I found you now, old rascal?" said he. "I've long been looking for you."

He was just going to take aim with his gun, when he bethought himself, "Perhaps the wolf has only swallowed granny, and she may yet be released;" therefore he did not shoot, but took a knife and began to cut open the sleeping wolf's maw.

When he had made several cuts, he saw a red hood gleam, and after one or two more cuts out skipped Red Hood, and cried, "Oh, how frightened I have been; it was so dark in the wolf's maw!"

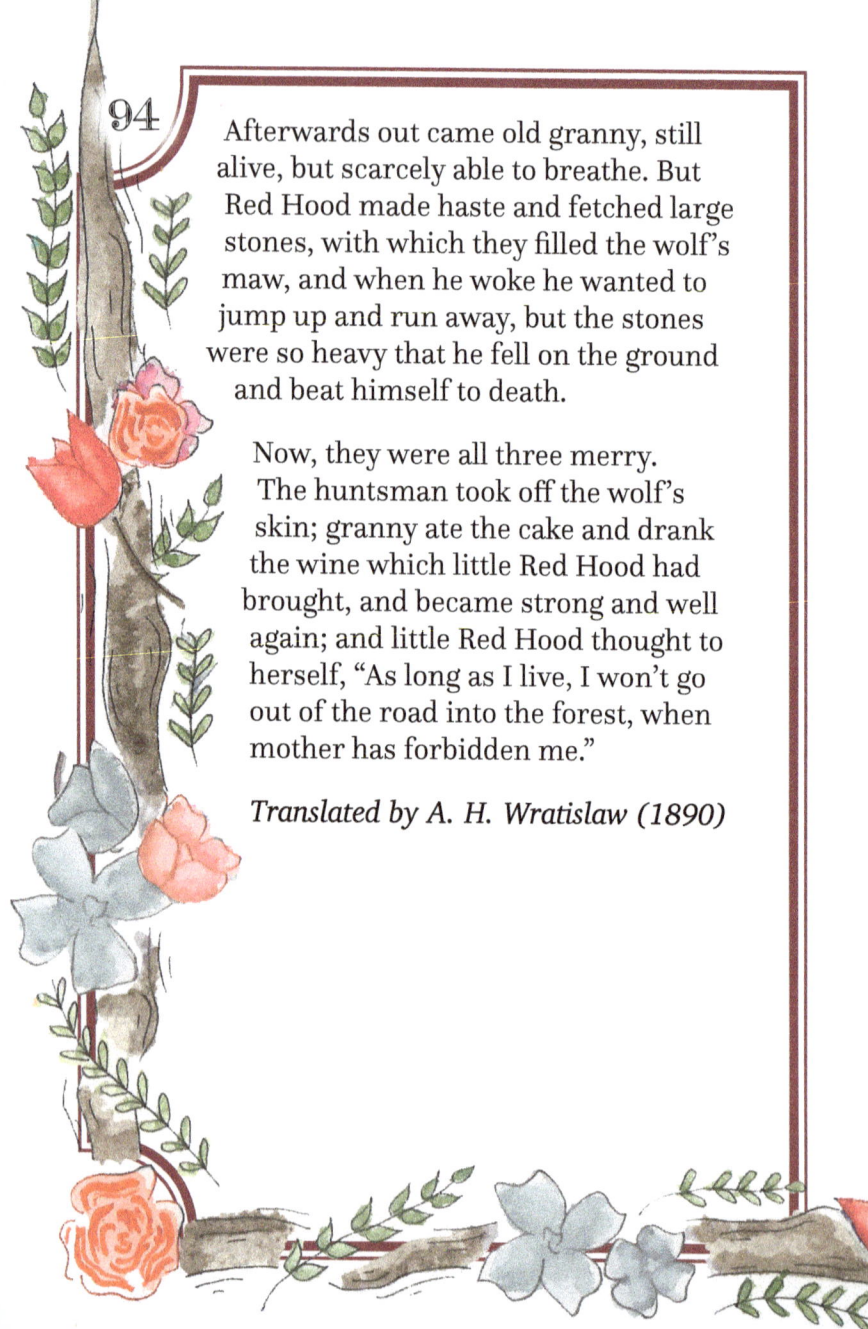

Afterwards out came old granny, still alive, but scarcely able to breathe. But Red Hood made haste and fetched large stones, with which they filled the wolf's maw, and when he woke he wanted to jump up and run away, but the stones were so heavy that he fell on the ground and beat himself to death.

Now, they were all three merry. The huntsman took off the wolf's skin; granny ate the cake and drank the wine which little Red Hood had brought, and became strong and well again; and little Red Hood thought to herself, "As long as I live, I won't go out of the road into the forest, when mother has forbidden me."

Translated by A. H. Wratislaw (1890)

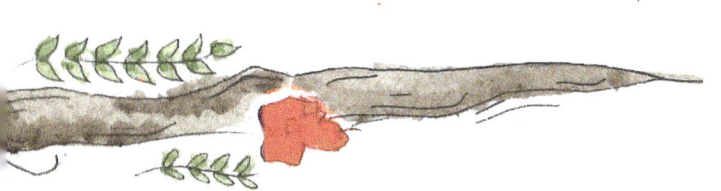

COMMENTS

The two most common dissimilarities in this story involve the ending: is Little Red rescued or not? In the 1867 Italian/Austrian version, called "Little Red Hat," and in Charles Perrault's French version from 1697, she is not. Perrault even writes this clear moral at the end of his tale: "Children, especially attractive, well bred young ladies, should never talk to strangers, for if they should do so, they may well provide dinner for a wolf. I say 'wolf,' but there are various kinds of wolves. There are also those who are charming, quiet, polite, unassuming, complacent, and sweet, who pursue young women at home and in the streets. And unfortunately, it is these gentle wolves who are the most dangerous ones of all." I admit I had a small giggle upon reading those lines, though they are completely true.

The 1889 Lower Lusatia (eastern German and western Poland region of today) and the 1857 Brothers Grimm version both introduce a hunter/woodcutter who saves Granny and Red; in these accounts Red comes up with her own life lesson: don't leave the path and wander into the woods if your mother has told you not to.

Red's nickname, which is given to her based on an important clothing item she always wears, varies throughout the stories as well. The Grimm retelling calls her "Little Red Cap" as she wears a hat made of red velvet. Charles Perrault's story carries the name that has remained the most popular: "Little Red Riding Hood." However, I have shared the Lower Lusatia version because 1) I enjoy Red's surviving her journey, unlike Perrault's tale, and learning her own life lesson rather than the reader having to learn from her death; 2) this version, unlike the Grimm tale, gives her the red hood she is so famously known for today; and 3) the Grimms have already been given a lot of credit in this book for their incredible contributions to the fairy tale genre.

In the several variations I read, all had a fiendish wolf, with the exception of the Italian/Austrian "Little Red Hat." This tale has an ogre who is overwhelmingly disgusting and disturbing in ways I don't care to share. Speaking of overwhelmingly disgusting and disturbing, folklorist Achille Millien collected a French version around 1870 called "The Grandmother" that is composed of multiple layers of unnerving features. I wouldn't consider my research of the story complete without having read both of these, but I also wouldn't recommend them to the young or faint of heart.

Despite those two disconcerting versions, in the end, this story, the sonnet I wrote for it, and Rehanna Mae's illustration have all combined to make this one of my fast favorite fairy tales. (You can probably tell by my extensive chattering on about it here.) I hope you've enjoyed it as well.

Rehanna Mae '16

The Mermaid

After the storms they found you, stranded in
a solitary pool of water. I
proposed they return you to the ocean;
they felt it their duty to civilize
you, though, and carried you far from your home
and into the Town, hiding your shimmer-
ing scales under the latest fashion, comb-
ing, taming, and covering your glimmer-
ing sea-green hair. And though you appeared to
acclimate yourself as best as you could,
abandoning those late-night attempts you
once made for freedom, your silence said you'd
never forget....When rains came heavily,
I swear I heard you singing for the sea.

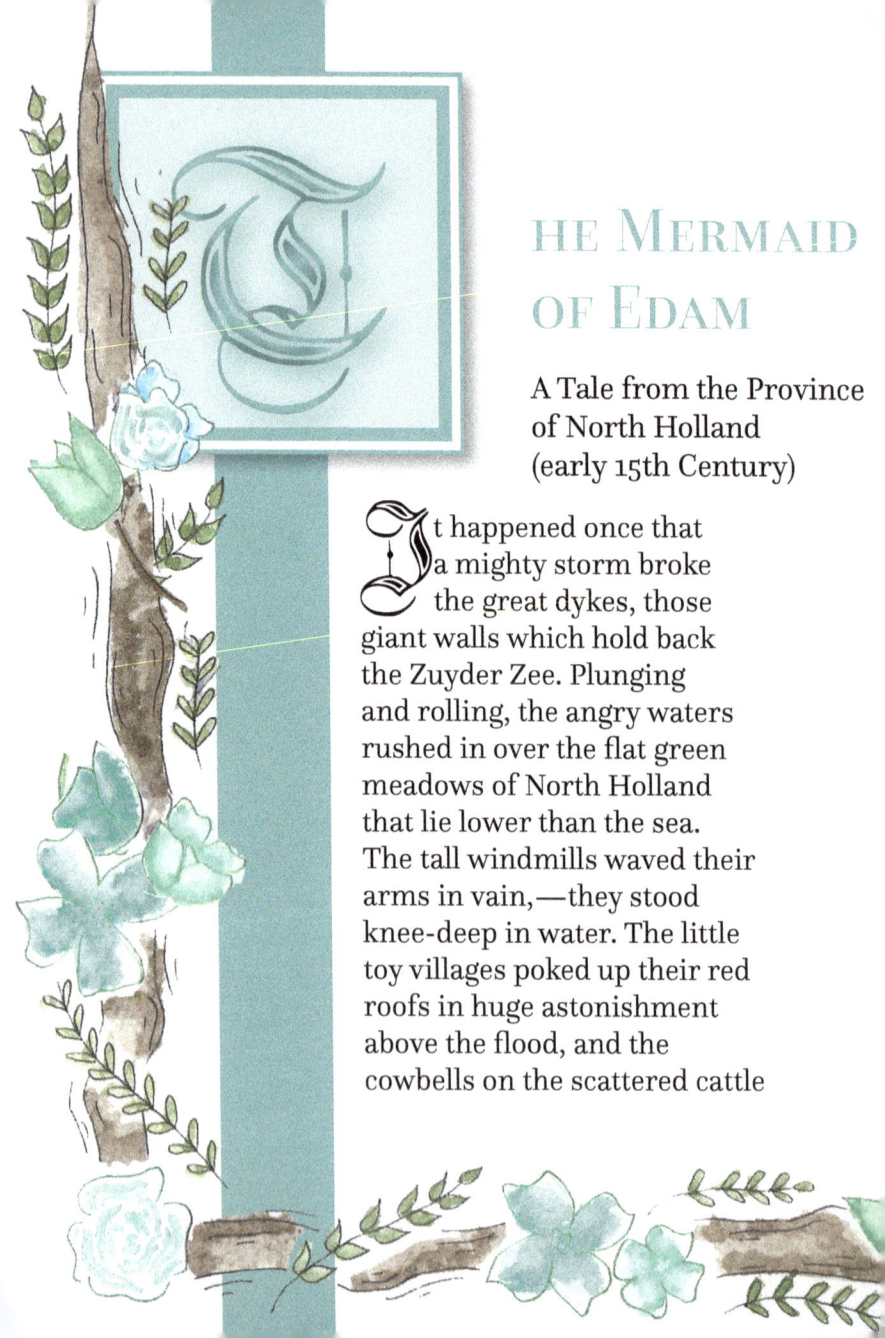

The Mermaid of Edam

A Tale from the Province of North Holland (early 15th Century)

It happened once that a mighty storm broke the great dykes, those giant walls which hold back the Zuyder Zee. Plunging and rolling, the angry waters rushed in over the flat green meadows of North Holland that lie lower than the sea. The tall windmills waved their arms in vain,—they stood knee-deep in water. The little toy villages poked up their red roofs in huge astonishment above the flood, and the cowbells on the scattered cattle rang out a wild tonka-tonka, discordant in alarm.

When the waves began to recede somewhat, and the green meadows showed themselves again, smiling in the sunlight, certain young lassies from the city of Edam set out to carry fresh water to the cows in the distant pastures, for the poor things had had nothing to drink for hours, with only salt-water about them. The girls were merrily splashing along through the puddles in their wooden shoes, carrying their pails on wooden yokes slung over their shoulders, when all of a sudden one of them cried:

"Look there! Look there!"

At that the lassies all stood still, and what should they see in a shallow pool before them, but a gleaming silver-green tail, floundering helplessly and churning up a shining shower of water.

"It's a great fish," cried one of the maids, "a fish, carried in by the flood!"

"It will never get back," said another, "for this pool is standing alone with no outlet to the sea!"

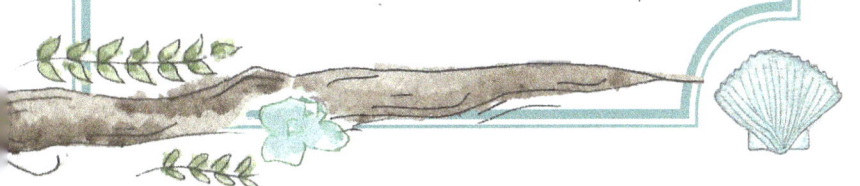

But just as they spoke, the third lass gave a shriek.

"O look, look! It's a mermaid!"

There, as sure as butter and cheese, rising from the water, appeared the dripping head and shoulders of a woman,—a beautiful woman with sea-green hair and the glistening tail of a fish!

The girls stood open-mouthed.

"What a curious thing!" whispered one. "Let's take her to the city."

All this time, the poor mermaid was struggling sadly with her arms to get out of the mud, hoping to reach a place where she could float and make her way back to the sea. It was beautiful where she lived far out on the sapphire waters. Her friends and loved ones were there, sporting with the waves. She must return. She must. But the bevy of Edam lassies surrounded her. Though she protested with all her might, they lifted her in their arms and carried her off to the town.

Past quiet, shady canals, by the huge towering Gothic Church, as solid as a fortress, they bore her struggling and straining, to the great Town Hall. And when the Burgomaster heard that a mermaid had been found you may well believe that he came to the Town Hall in a hurry, in as much of a hurry, that is, as his dignity would permit him. And the town-councillors came likewise, and crowds and crowds of people—for Edam was a great city in those days, the water gate to Amsterdam, with twenty-five thousand burghers: and as many of that twenty-five thousand as could walk or run or hobble, came clumping and clattering to see the marvelous wonder cast up for them by the sea.

First they fed the mermaid and treated her very kindly, till they stopped her wild struggling and put her at her ease. Then they set about in proper manner debating what they should do with her.

The Burgomaster was of opinion that a mermaid could not be permitted to remain a mermaid in Edam. A mermaid was a wild, fantastical creature, savoring too much of Fairyland.

She had no place in a sober, substantial city like Edam.

Now, you must know that the burghers of Edam have little to do with mermaids and giants and fairies. They live in a placid and beautiful country and are content with the world as it is. What need have they to go building castles in the air, or riding the horses of fancy to the moon? Leave it to the poor folk of the barren heath or fen-country to the northward and eastward, in Drente or thereabouts, to run off to Fairyland and have dealings with elves and earthmen and giants. Their own land is poor enough. No wonder at times they must needs run away on the fluttering wings of fancy. Not so with North Holland, ah, no, indeed! North Holland is rich and green and satisfying as it is. No need to fly away from North Holland on a wild goose chase into the clouds! So say the people of Edam. North Holland is the Land-of-Reality, the Land-of-things-as-they-are, the country of markets and black and white cows! And Edam, ah, Edam is the city of cheese, famed to the uttermost ends of the earth for the glories of its cheese. In such a place, pray tell, what room was there for a mermaid?

The Burgomaster gazed upon the coat-of-arms of Edam, hanging on the wall before him, and he was well pleased that it was adorned with no griffin or dragon or such-like fantastical monster. It bore the figure of a fine, sleek, fighting steer, with no nonsense whatever about him, and as the Burgomaster looked, he exclaimed with great solemnity:

"We cannot let a mermaid remain a mermaid in Edam. There is only one thing to do. We must make her over into a useful Edam housewife!"

"But,—" cried a very young town-councillor, with a flash of inspiration, "why not take her back and put her in the sea?"

The Burgomaster was shocked. Impressively, he replied:

"Nay. that would be shirking our bounden duty. If we put her in the sea, the poor thing will remain always a mermaid and never be anything better. Since she has been brought to us, we must civilize her and make her like

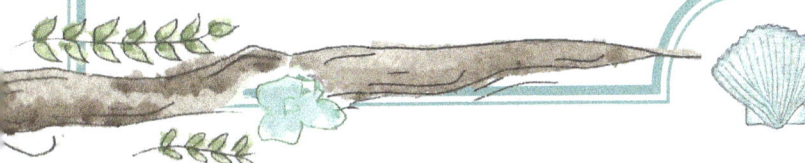

ourselves. We must turn her into a good burgher-vrouw with no absurd nonsense about her."

"But," objected the young town-councillor. "Maybe she wasn't meant to be a good burgher-vrouw. Perhaps it isn't in her nature to be a burgher-vrouw. Perhaps she was meant to be a mermaid and sport in the water. Who are we, that we should try to make her like ourselves? Would it not be best to put her back in the sea?"

But the Burgomaster and the older men frowned sternly on the young fellow and thought him a silly booby who was greatly in need of years and gray hair to bring him wisdom. If he did not know that to be like the burghers of Edam was the height of desirable glories, then he had a great deal to learn, the poor, unfortunate simpleton! Who were they, indeed!

So it was agreed by the city council,—they would make the mermaid over into a proper Edam housewife.

Well, they didn't ask permission of the mermaid, but they dressed her up in robes of the finest fashion then in vogue in the city, and they did their best to cover her long green tail from sight. Every now and then, however, the outlandish thing would show itself below her voluminous petticoats. As to her tell-tale hair with the sea-green sheen like waves flung up by the west-wind, why they hid that beneath a white lace cap. All was of the very best style and quality, you may be sure of that.

And when the mermaid was installed in a good substantial townhouse, the women of the city came by turns to teach her to sew and to spin, and to churn the cheese which is the pride of Edam. They taught her to work, work, work, to save, save, save, and to take such pride in cleanliness, that she could not endure so much as the smallest speck of dirt. They provided her too, with a stout and buxom servant lass, who scrubbed from morning till night,—pots, pans, windows, hearth, doorstep, sidewalk, housefront,—yes, even the neat red bricks of the street before the door,—scrub, scrub, scrub! And what would you have?

With teaching like this, the mermaid was quite made over. She

sewed, she spun, she churned, she looked after her servant lass, and kept her eternally scrubbing.

But sometimes there came memories and a longing upon the mermaid. She longed for the water again. She longed to play with wind and wave, to fly with the flying-fish, leap with the dolphins. She longed for her little home of shells amid a forest of sea-weed. She longed to lie lazily and sun herself on the rocks. She longed for her old free life among mermen and mermaidens,— that happy, carefree life that had nothing to do with scrubbing, nothing to do with saving, nothing to do with cheese.

Then she would tear off her clothes and wriggle away toward the sea. Aye, at such times it took two strong men to keep her from jumping into the water! It took two strong men to bring her back to the city.

They were very patient with her, very courteous, very kindly, the sturdy burghers of Edam, but they kept unswervingly to their purpose, plodding on and on and on. So, bye-and-bye, they accomplished their end, and crushed all the nonsense out of her. She no longer tried to run away. She became a proper burgher-vrouw, who sewed and spun and churned. Then all the good folk of Edam congratulated themselves.

"We have done a fine work," said they, "to make a mermaid over into a housewife like ourselves." Only sometimes a child, a very young child, would come and sit before the strange woman with a question in his eyes. She knew something he wanted to know, something the burghers of Edam could not tell him. Ah, if she would only speak, she could carry him off to a beautiful land, a free, a glorious, a golden land, where dreams are the only truth.

But alack! the mermaid never spoke. This one thing the burghers of Edam could not accomplish. They could not make her speak Dutch! No, that they could not bring about. They could not make her speak Dutch! And so she never told her secrets to the children.

But one day the Burgomaster came, in condescending glory, to pay an afternoon call and delight his eyes with a sight of the good

work done by the burghers, for which he took no small amount of credit to himself. Important, pompous, proud, he stood on the mermaid's threshold.

"Now," he thought. "I shall see how greatly we have improved this poor, silly, flighty creature!"

With that, the servant lass opened the door, and the Burgomaster requested her to lead him to her mistress. And now, from an inner room, the mermaid saw the visitor. Her servant had just scrubbed the floor, which was white as driven snow, and had the mermaid not become a proper Edam housewife? Would any Edam housewife permit a Burgomaster to soil the fresh-scoured planks by trampling them with his boots? She waved a sign to her servant, who straightway picked the Burgomaster up bodily in her arms. Ah, the poor old fellow! How painfully he was astounded! How helplessly he kicked his legs! How wounded was his dignity! She bore him to a chair on the opposite side of the hall. Then, without aye, yes, or no, she set him down, kerplunk, as though he had been a baby; she took off his boots; she put a pair of slippers on his feet; and when she had thus prepared him, she led him across to her mistress. Thus was the Burgomaster rewarded for civilizing a mermaid.

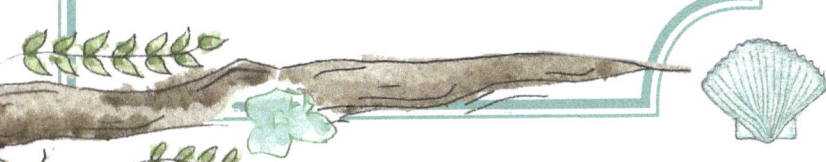

COMMENTS

Mermaids have captured the imaginations of man since far back into our history. Their roots are generally traced to mythology, in which certain gods appear with human torsos and fish tails.

Modern movies about mermaids reflect the same questions ancient stories posed: 1) Are mermaids real? 2) Are they good or bad? 3) How does man react to them? 4) How do they interact with man? "The Mermaid of Edam" was one I hadn't heard growing up, but I appreciate how this story answers each of those questions.

When the mermaid is discovered, she is considered not "bad" but savage and in need of refinement. Refinement means, of course, covering up everything that defines her true self. Her reaction is silent obedience (aside from those early attempts to get home again). When her hair and scales are covered, she covers her song and her voice as well—allowing man none of her since he refuses to accept her.

An element I added from other tales is my mermaid's song. Of course "The Little Mermaid" by Andersen as well as the

Disney film version both grant their title character with a beautiful and charming singing voice ("The Little Mermaid"). A Northern Ireland story tells of a mermaid whose constant singing leads to her capture ("Mermaid"). The Sirens of mythology (sometimes pictured as mermaids) use their powerful song to drive men to their deaths. So my lonely mermaid sings when no one is listening, a symbol that her longing for home and her real essence cannot be completely taken from her.

This sad Dutch story brings a new perspective to the old myths. Why are we so excited by the prospects of the mythical and enchanting while also so ready to debase it, to change it to the normal we are more comfortable with? Fairy tales in general, and this one in particular, are a call for readers to open themselves up to a chance at enchantment and a reminder never to cover up these chances with our comfort in the commonplace.

Rehanna Mae '16

Thumbelina

One lonely wish for a little love stirred
a kindly witch to share her magic bar-
ley-corn, which, when planted, grew blooms that spurred
a mother's kiss. This blossom birthed by far
the smallest, the loveliest of girls whose
looks and lyrics caused quite the commotion
of devotion; an old toad stole our Muse
to be her frog-son's fiancée; then one
event after the other brought hopeful
beaux, such as a crafty beetle and a
mole king, until the swallow she carefully saved, saved her, and our Thumbelina
met a flower prince and earned wedding wings;
her swallow told me so I'd share these things.

HUMBELINA

Hans Christian Andersen
(1835)

Once upon a time there was a woman who very much wanted to have a little tiny child, but didn't know where she could get one from; so she went to an old witch and said to her: "I do so want to have a little child; will you kindly tell me where I can get one?"

"Oh, we can manage that," said the witch, "there's a barleycorn for you! It isn't the kind that grows in the farmers' fields or that the chickens have to eat;

just put it in a flower-pot, and you shall
see what you shall see."

"Much obliged," said the woman, and gave the
witch twelve pence, and went home and planted
the barleycorn; and very soon a fine large flower
came up which looked just like a tulip, but the
petals were closed up tight as if it were still a
bud.

"That's a charming flower," said the woman, and
gave it a kiss on its pretty red and yellow petals.
But just as she kissed it the flower gave a loud
crack and opened. You could see it was a real
tulip, only right in the middle of it, on the green
stool that is there, sat a tiny little girl, as delicate
and pretty as could be. She was only a thumb-
joint long, so she was called Thumbelina. She
was given a splendid lacquered walnut shell for
a cradle, blue violet leaves for mattresses, and a
rose-leaf for a counterpane. There she slept at
night, but in the daytime she played about on the
table, where the woman had put a plate, round
which she put a whole wreath of flowers with
their stalks in the water; and on the water floated
a large tulip-leaf on which Thumbelina could sit
and sail from one side of the plate to the other.
She had two white horse-hairs to row with. It
was really beautiful to see her; she could

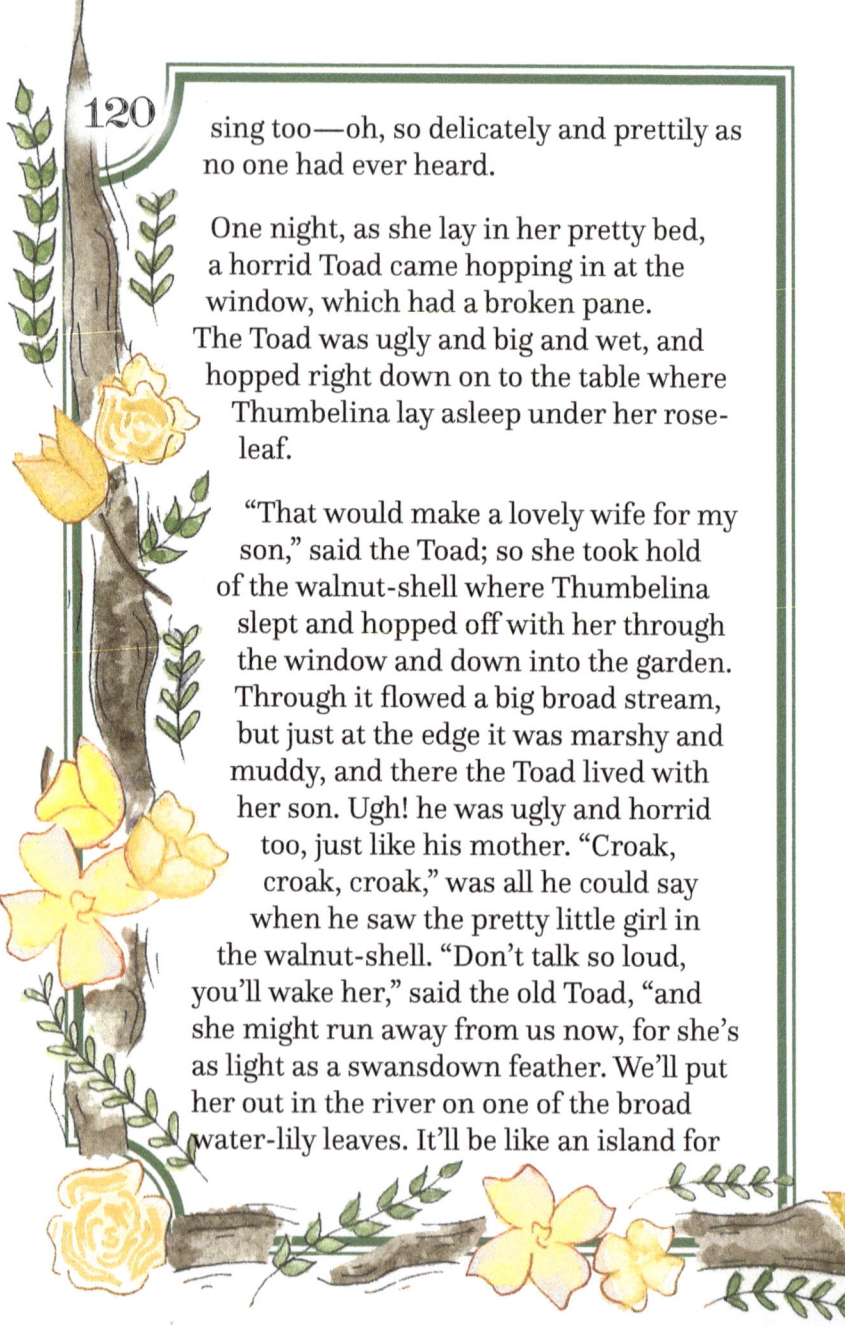

sing too—oh, so delicately and prettily as
no one had ever heard.

One night, as she lay in her pretty bed,
a horrid Toad came hopping in at the
window, which had a broken pane.
The Toad was ugly and big and wet, and
hopped right down on to the table where
Thumbelina lay asleep under her rose-
leaf.

"That would make a lovely wife for my
son," said the Toad; so she took hold
of the walnut-shell where Thumbelina
slept and hopped off with her through
the window and down into the garden.
Through it flowed a big broad stream,
but just at the edge it was marshy and
muddy, and there the Toad lived with
her son. Ugh! he was ugly and horrid
too, just like his mother. "Croak,
croak, croak," was all he could say
when he saw the pretty little girl in
the walnut-shell. "Don't talk so loud,
you'll wake her," said the old Toad, "and
she might run away from us now, for she's
as light as a swansdown feather. We'll put
her out in the river on one of the broad
water-lily leaves. It'll be like an island for

her, she's so little and light. She can run about there while we get the drawing-room under the mud ready for you two to make your home in."

There were a great many water-lilies growing out in the stream, with broad green leaves that looked as if they were floating on the water; and the leaf that was furthest out was also the biggest of all. To this leaf the old Toad swam out and put the walnut-shell with Thumbelina on it. The poor little wretch woke up very early in the morning, and when she saw where she was, she began to cry—oh, so bitterly!—for there was water all round the big leaf and she couldn't possibly get to land.

The old Toad stayed down in the mud and set about decorating her room with rushes and yellow water-lily buds, so as to make it nice and neat for her new daughter-in-law; and then she swam out with her ugly son to the leaf where Thumbelina stood; they were going to fetch her pretty bed and put it up in the bridal chamber before she came there herself. The old Toad curtsied low in the water before her and said: "I present my son to you. He is going to be your husband, and you will have a delightful life with him down in the mud."

"Croak, croak, croak," was all the son could say.

So they took the beautiful little bed and swam off with it while Thumbelina sat all alone on the green leaf crying, for she didn't want to live with the horrid Toad or have her ugly son for a husband. The little fishes, swimming beneath in the water, had seen the Toad and heard what she said, so they put their heads up; they wanted to see the little girl. But as soon as they saw her, they thought her so pretty that it grieved them very much to think that she had to go down to the ugly Toad. No, that could never be. So they swarmed together down in the water, all round the green stalk that held the leaf she was on, and gnawed it through with their teeth; so the leaf went floating down the stream, and bore Thumbelina far, far away, where the Toad could not go. Thumbelina sailed past many places, and the little birds in the bushes saw her and sang, "What a pretty little maid!" The leaf floated further and further away with her, and thus it was that Thumbelina went on her travels.

A beautiful little white butterfly kept flying round her, and at last settled on the leaf, for it took a fancy to Thumbelina, and she was very happy, for now the Toad could not get at her, and everything was beautiful where she was sailing: the sun shone on the water and made it glitter like gold. She took her sash and tied one end of it to the butterfly, and the other end she fastened to the leaf, and it went along much faster with her, for of course she was standing on the leaf. Just then a large Cockchafer came flying by and caught sight of her, and in an instant he had grasped her slender body in his claws, and flew up into a tree with her. But the green leaf went floating downstream and the butterfly with it, for he was tied to the leaf and could not get loose.

Goodness! How frightened poor Thumbelina was when the Cockchafer flew up into the tree with her. But she was most of all grieved for the pretty white butterfly which she had tied to the leaf, for unless it got loose it would be starved to death. However, the Cockchafer cared nothing about that. He alighted with her on the largest green leaf on the tree, and gave her honey out of the flowers to eat, and told her she was very

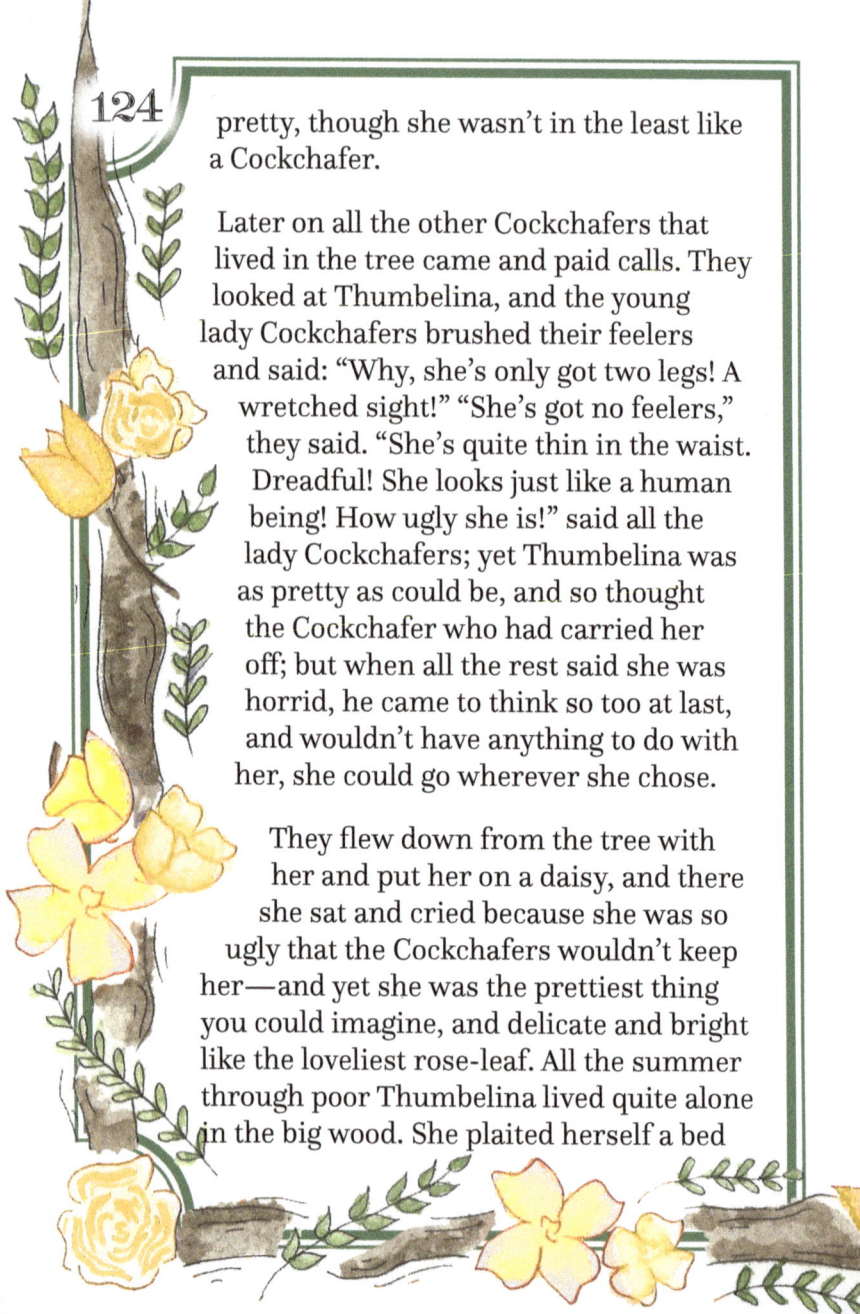

pretty, though she wasn't in the least like a Cockchafer.

Later on all the other Cockchafers that lived in the tree came and paid calls. They looked at Thumbelina, and the young lady Cockchafers brushed their feelers and said: "Why, she's only got two legs! A wretched sight!" "She's got no feelers," they said. "She's quite thin in the waist. Dreadful! She looks just like a human being! How ugly she is!" said all the lady Cockchafers; yet Thumbelina was as pretty as could be, and so thought the Cockchafer who had carried her off; but when all the rest said she was horrid, he came to think so too at last, and wouldn't have anything to do with her, she could go wherever she chose.

They flew down from the tree with her and put her on a daisy, and there she sat and cried because she was so ugly that the Cockchafers wouldn't keep her—and yet she was the prettiest thing you could imagine, and delicate and bright like the loveliest rose-leaf. All the summer through poor Thumbelina lived quite alone in the big wood. She plaited herself a bed

of green stalks and hung it up under a
large dock leaf so as to be out of the rain.
She picked the honey out of the flowers
and ate it, and she drank the dew, which lay
every morning on the leaves. There she spent
the summer and the autumn; but then came
winter, the long cold winter. All the birds that
had sung so prettily to her, flew their way; the
trees and flowers withered, and the big dock-
leaf under which she had lived rolled up and
turned to nothing but a yellow dry stalk, and she
was terribly cold, for her clothes were in rags,
and she herself was so little and delicate. Poor
Thumbelina! She was like to be frozen to death!
Then it began to snow, and every snowflake that
fell on her was just as when anybody throws a
whole shovelful on any of us—for we are big,
and Thumbelina was only an inch high. So she
wrapped herself up in a dead leaf, but there was
no warmth in it, and she shivered with the cold.

Just outside the wood where she was now, lay a
large cornfield, but the corn had long been off
it, and only the bare dry stubble stuck out of the
frozen ground. This was like a whole forest for
her to get through, and oh! how she did shiver
with cold! At last she came to a Fieldmouse's
door, which was a little hole down among

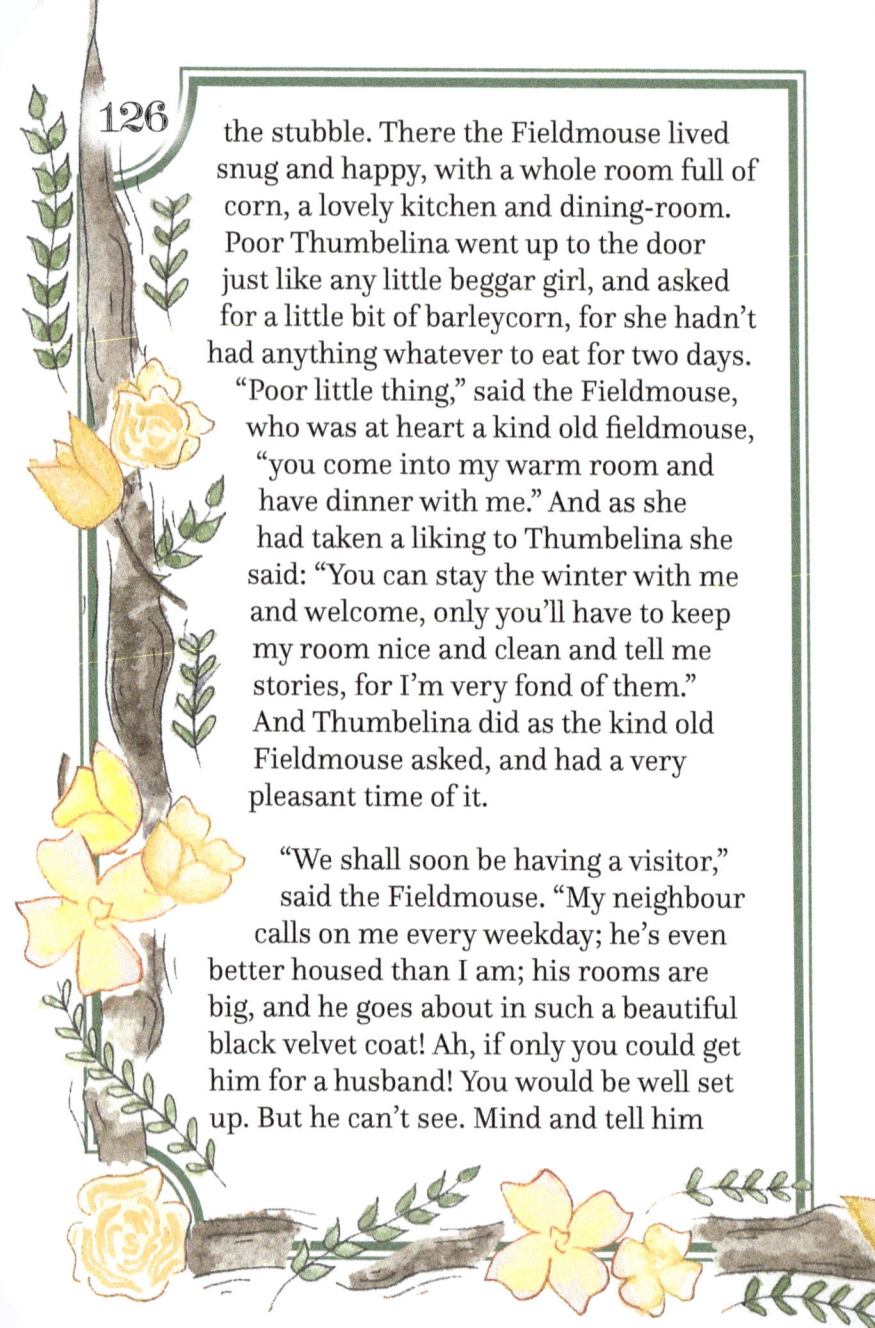

the stubble. There the Fieldmouse lived snug and happy, with a whole room full of corn, a lovely kitchen and dining-room. Poor Thumbelina went up to the door just like any little beggar girl, and asked for a little bit of barleycorn, for she hadn't had anything whatever to eat for two days.

"Poor little thing," said the Fieldmouse, who was at heart a kind old fieldmouse, "you come into my warm room and have dinner with me." And as she had taken a liking to Thumbelina she said: "You can stay the winter with me and welcome, only you'll have to keep my room nice and clean and tell me stories, for I'm very fond of them." And Thumbelina did as the kind old Fieldmouse asked, and had a very pleasant time of it.

"We shall soon be having a visitor," said the Fieldmouse. "My neighbour calls on me every weekday; he's even better housed than I am; his rooms are big, and he goes about in such a beautiful black velvet coat! Ah, if only you could get him for a husband! You would be well set up. But he can't see. Mind and tell him

the very prettiest stories you know!"
But Thumbelina didn't care much
about this—she didn't want to marry the
neighbour, for he was a Mole. He came and
paid a call in his black velvet coat. He was very
well off and very learned, the Fieldmouse said
his mansion was more than twenty times the
size of hers, and he was very well informed; but
he didn't like the sun and the pretty flowers,
and abused them, for he had never seen them.
Thumbelina had to sing, and she sang both
"Cockchafer, Cockchafer fly away home" and also
"The monk walked in the meadow," and the Mole
fell in love with her for her pretty voice; but said
nothing about it, for he was a very cautious man.

He had recently dug a big passage through the
earth from his house to theirs, and gave the
Fieldmouse and Thumbelina leave to walk there
whenever they liked; but he begged them not
to be frightened at the dead bird that lay in the
passage—a whole bird with beak and feathers
which had certainly been dead only a little time,
at the beginning of the winter, and was now
buried just where he had made his passage.

The Mole took a bit of touchwood in his mouth
(for that shines like fire in the dark) and went
in front and lighted them along through

the long dark passage, and when they got to where the dead bird lay, the Mole pushed his broad back against the ceiling and lifted the earth so that there was a big hole which let in the light: in the middle of this floor lay a dead swallow with its pretty wings close against its sides and its legs and head down in among its feathers: the poor bird had certainly died of cold. Thumbelina was very sorry for it; she was fond of all the little birds that had sung and twittered so prettily to her all the summer long; but the Mole kicked it with his short leg and said: "He won't be squeaking any more! It must be wretched to be born a little bird! Thank God, none of my children will be like that. A bird has nothing but its twit, twit, and is bound to starve to death in winter."

"Yes, you may well say so as a reasonable man," said the Fieldmouse; "what has the bird to show for all its twit, twit, when winter comes? Why, it has to starve and freeze, and yet they're so proud about it!"

Thumbelina said nothing, but when the

others turned their backs on the bird, she stooped down and parted the feathers that covered its head, and kissed its dead eyes. "Perhaps this was the one that sang to me so prettily in the summer," she thought; "what a lot of pleasure it gave me, the dear little bird."

The Mole now stopped up the hole through which the daylight shone in, and saw the ladies home. But that night Thumbelina couldn't sleep at all, so she got out of bed and plaited a nice large coverlet of hay, and carried it down and spread it about the dead bird, and then she laid some soft cotton wool she had found in the Fieldmouse's room, on the bird's sides, so that it might lie warmly on the cold ground. "Farewell, you pretty little bird," said she; "farewell, and thank you for your lovely singing in the summer, when all the trees were green and the sun shone so hot on us." She laid her head against the bird's heart, and got quite a fright all at once, for it seemed as if something was knocking inside! It was the bird's heart. The bird was not dead; it was only in a swoon, and now that it was warmed, it came to life again.

In autumn, you know, all the swallows fly away to the warm countries, but if there is one that lags behind it gets frozen so that it tumbles

down quite dead and lies where it fell, and the cold snow covers it over.

Thumbelina really shivered, so frightened was she: for the bird was enormously big compared with her who was only an inch high: but she took courage and laid the cotton wool closer about the poor swallow, and folded a peppermint leaf, that she had for her own counterpane, and put it over the bird's head. Next night she stole down to it again, and this time it was quite alive, but so weak that it could only open its eyes for a second, and look at Thumbelina who stood there with a bit of touchwood in her hand, for other light she had none.

"Thank you, you pretty little child," the sick swallow said to her, "I've been beautifully warmed. Soon I shall get back my strength and be able to fly about again in the warm sun outside."

"Oh," said Thumbelina, "but it's dreadfully cold outside, snowing and freezing! You must stay in your warm bed, I'll nurse you, be sure!" Then she brought the swallow some water in the leaf of a plant, and it drank, and told her how it had hurt its wing on a thorn bush, and so couldn't fly as well as the other swallows when they set out to fly, far, far away to the warm countries. At last it had fallen to the ground, but it couldn't remember any more and didn't know in the least how it had got to where it was.

All the winter it stayed down there, and Thumbelina was very kind to it, and got very fond of it, but neither the Mole nor the Fieldmouse heard anything whatever about it; they disliked the poor wretched swallow.

As soon as spring came and the sun's warmth got into the ground, the swallow said good-bye to Thumbelina, who opened the hole, which the Mole had made above. The sun shone in delightfully, and the swallow asked if Thumbelina would not come with it: she could sit on its back and they would fly away into the greenwood. But Thumbelina knew that it would grieve the old Fieldmouse, if she left her like that. "No, I can't," said Thumbelina. "Good-bye, good-bye, you kind pretty maid," said the swallow, and flew out into the sunshine. Thumbelina stood looking after it, and the

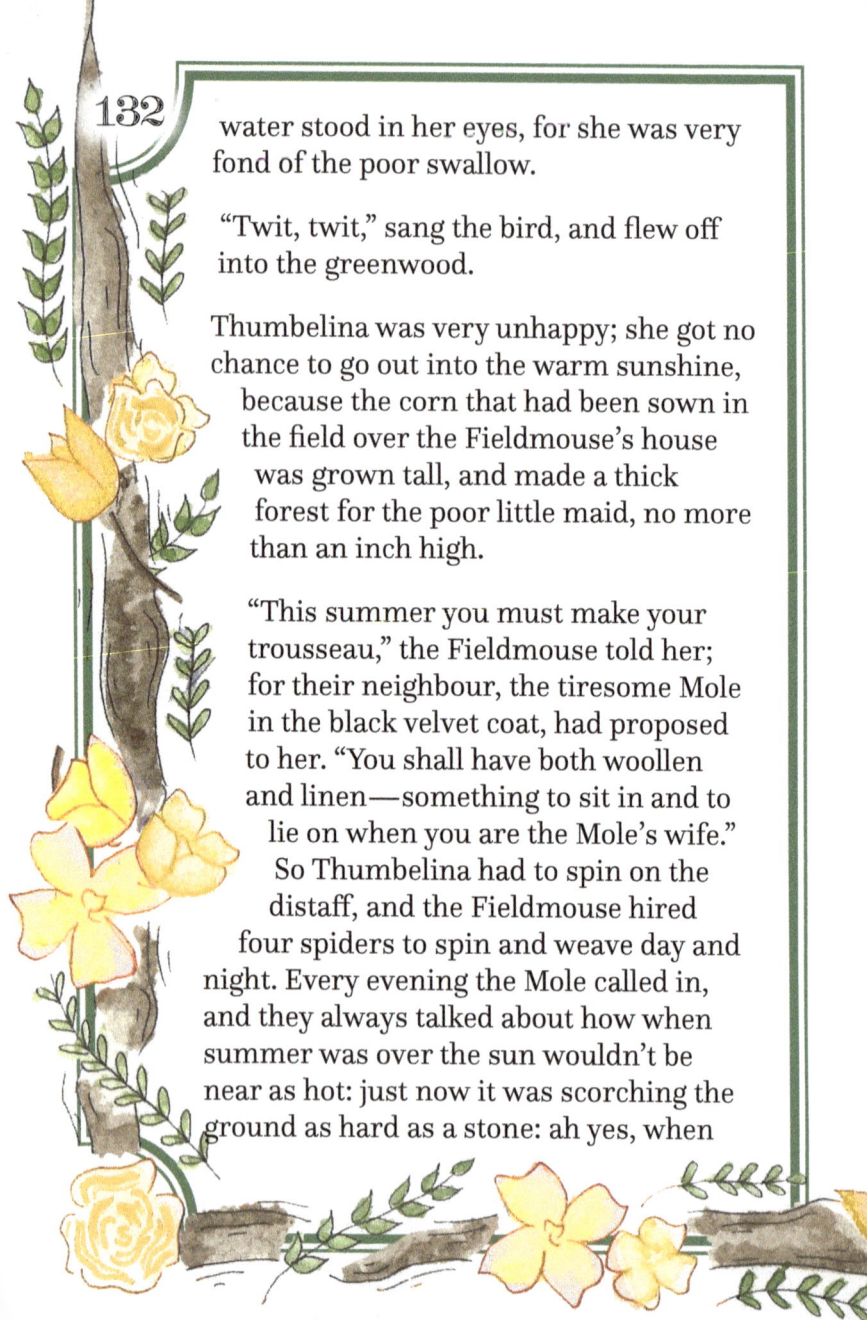

water stood in her eyes, for she was very
fond of the poor swallow.

"Twit, twit," sang the bird, and flew off
into the greenwood.

Thumbelina was very unhappy; she got no
chance to go out into the warm sunshine,
because the corn that had been sown in
the field over the Fieldmouse's house
was grown tall, and made a thick
forest for the poor little maid, no more
than an inch high.

"This summer you must make your
trousseau," the Fieldmouse told her;
for their neighbour, the tiresome Mole
in the black velvet coat, had proposed
to her. "You shall have both woollen
and linen—something to sit in and to
lie on when you are the Mole's wife."
So Thumbelina had to spin on the
distaff, and the Fieldmouse hired
four spiders to spin and weave day and
night. Every evening the Mole called in,
and they always talked about how when
summer was over the sun wouldn't be
near as hot: just now it was scorching the
ground as hard as a stone: ah yes, when

the summer was over Thumbelina
should be married. But she wasn't at all
pleased; she didn't like the tiresome Mole
one bit. Every morning when the sun rose and
every evening when it set she stole out to the
doorway, and there, when the wind parted the
heads of corn, so that she could see the blue sky,
she thought how bright and pretty it was outside,
and longed to get another sight of the dear
swallow: but he never came, he must certainly
be flying far away in the beautiful greenwood. By
the time autumn came, Thumbelina had all her
trousseau ready.

"In four weeks' time you shall be married," the
Fieldmouse told her, but Thumbelina cried
and said she wouldn't marry the tiresome
Mole. "Rubbish," said the Fieldmouse, "don't be
pigheaded or I'll bite you with my white teeth.
It's a splendid husband you're getting. The queen
herself hasn't the like of his black velvet coat;
and a full kitchen and cellar he has, too! Just you
thank your Maker for him."

So the wedding was to be; already the Mole had
come to fetch Thumbelina, and with him she
must go deep down underground, and never
come out into the warm sun, for he couldn't
stand it. The poor child was bitterly

grieved, for now she must bid farewell to the beautiful sunshine, which she had at least had the chance of seeing from the Fieldmouse's door.

"Farewell! Farewell! bright sun," she said, stretching her arms upwards and stepping a little way outside the Fieldmouse's house, for now the corn was reaped, and only the dry stubble left. "Farewell! Farewell!" she said again, and threw her arms about a little red flower that grew there. "Give my love to the dear swallow for me if ever you see him."

Twit! Twit! sounded at that moment above her head. She looked up and there was the swallow just flying by. He was overjoyed when he caught sight of Thumbelina, and she told him how she hated to have the ugly Mole for a husband, and how she must live right down underground where the sun never shone. She couldn't help crying.

"Cold winter is coming," said the swallow. "I am going to fly far away to the warm countries, will you come with me? You can sit on my back, only tie yourself tight with your sash, and we'll fly far away from the ugly Mole and his dark home, far over the mountains to the warm countries where the sun shines fairer than here, and there is always summer and lovely flowers. Do fly away with me, you sweet little Thumbelina, who saved my life when I lay frozen in that dark cellar underground."

"Yes, I will come with you," said Thumbelina. So she got up on the bird's back, put her feet upon his outspread wings, tied her belt fast to one of his strongest feathers, and off flew the swallow high in the air over forest and lake, high above the great mountains where the snow always lies, and where Thumbelina might have frozen in the cold air but that she crept in among the bird's warm feathers, and only put her little head out to see all the beauty beneath her.

At last they got to the warm countries. There the sun shone far brighter than here, the sky seemed twice as high, and on hedges and ditches grew the loveliest clusters of grapes, green and purple. In the woods grew oranges and lemons, there was a scent of myrtle and mint, and in the roads pretty children ran about and played with great gay butterflies. But the swallow flew still farther, and the country grew more and more delightful. Under splendid trees, beside a blue lake, stood a shining palace of white marble, built in ancient days, with creepers twining about its tall pillars. At its top were a number of swallows' nests, one of which was the home of the swallow who was carrying Thumbelina.

"Here is my house," said the swallow, "but won't you look out for yourself one of the finest of the flowers that grow down below? And I'll put you there, and you shall find everything as happy as your heart can wish."

"That will be lovely," said she, and clapped her little hands.

A great white marble column lay there, which had fallen down and broken into three pieces: between them grew large beautiful white flowers. The swallow flew down with Thumbelina and set her on one of the broad leaves. But what a surprise for her! A little man was sitting in the middle of the flower, as white and transparent as if he were made of glass, with the prettiest gold crown on his head and the loveliest bright wings

on his shoulders, and he was no bigger
than Thumbelina. He was the angel of
the flower. In each of them there lived such
another little man or woman, but this one was
the king of them all.

"Goodness, how beautiful he is," Thumbelina
whispered to the swallow. The little prince
was quite alarmed by the swallow, which was a
giant bird to him, tiny and delicate as he was,
but when he saw Thumbelina he was delighted,
for she was by far the prettiest girl he had ever
seen. He took his gold crown off his head and
laid it upon hers, asked what her name was,
and whether she would be his wife, for then she
would become queen of all the flowers. Here
indeed was a husband—very different from
the Toad's son or the Mole with his black velvet
coat. So she said "Yes" to the handsome prince;
and out of every flower there came a lady or
a lord, so pretty that it was a pleasure to see
them. Everyone brought Thumbelina a present,
but the best of all was a pair of beautiful wings
taken from a big white fly. They were fastened to
Thumbelina's back, and then she could fly from
flower to flower. There were great rejoicings,
and the swallow sat on his nest up there and
sang to them as well as ever he could; but at

heart he was sad, for he was very fond of Thumbelina and would have liked never to be parted from her. "You shan't be called Thumbelina," the angel of the flower said to her; "it's an ugly name, and you are very pretty; we will call you Maia."

"Good-bye, good-bye," said the swallow, when he flew back, away from the warm countries; far, far, back to Denmark. There he had a little nest above the window, where the man who can tell stories lives; and to him he sang, "Twit, twit," and that's the way we came by the whole story.

Translated by M.R. James (1930)

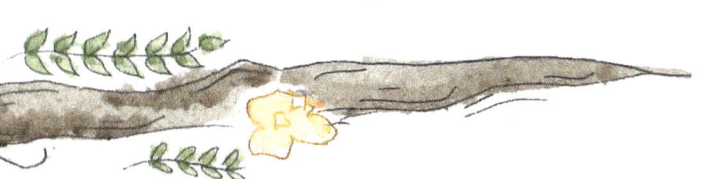

COMMENTS

Something I find quite interesting about any story is the reason behind and method of how it is being told; in other words, how is the reader or listener receiving the tale? For "Thumbelina," the ending explains exactly this: one of the central characters, the swallow, nests outside the house of a fairy tale author. Perhaps this is Andersen's way of writing himself into the story, or perhaps it is just an interesting way to end and explain how we know about Tiny.

Speaking of "Tiny," though one version says she is called by both names, "Tiny" is more often used, yet "Thumbelina" is more often recognized today and consistently used in the translation provided here. Whatever her name, three essential qualities remain: her beauty, her size, and her song. She is rewarded for her kindness with love (the bird and her prince), freedom (the wedding wings), and immortality (the written story).

Rehanna Mae '16

The Happy Prince

High above the city stood a statue
of the happy prince. One winter night a
swallow stalled between his feet en route to
southern warmth, and there felt tear drops from the
sapphire eyes. "Who are you?" "The Happy Prince."
"Then tell me why you cry?" "Because from here,
I see my city's sorrow. Help me since
I cannot move myself." And though the dear
bird feared the coming cold he picked away
the sapphires, ruby, and gold covering
the prince, at his command, and shared with frayed
mothers, writers, daughters. When fluttering
wings froze, the shineless prince and bird, love-bold,
were flown to the Lasting City of Gold.

The Happy Prince

Oscar Wilde (1888)

High above the city, on a tall column, stood the statue of the Happy Prince. He was gilded all over with thin leaves of fine gold, for eyes he had two bright sapphires, and a large red ruby glowed on his sword-hilt.

He was very much admired indeed. "He is as beautiful as a weathercock," remarked one of the Town Councillors who wished to gain a reputation for having artistic tastes; "only not quite so useful," he added, fearing lest people should think him unpractical, which he really was not.

"Why can't you be like the Happy Prince?" asked a sensible mother of her little boy who was crying for the moon. "The Happy Prince never dreams of crying for anything."

"I am glad there is some one in the world who is quite happy," muttered a disappointed man as he gazed at the wonderful statue.

"He looks just like an angel," said the Charity Children as they came out of the cathedral in their bright scarlet cloaks and their clean white pinafores.

"How do you know?" said the Mathematical Master, "you have never seen one."

"Ah! but we have, in our dreams," answered the children; and the Mathematical Master frowned and looked very severe, for he did not approve of children dreaming.

One night there flew over the city a little Swallow. His friends had gone away to Egypt six weeks before, but he had stayed behind for he was in love with the most beautiful Reed. He had met her early in the spring as he was

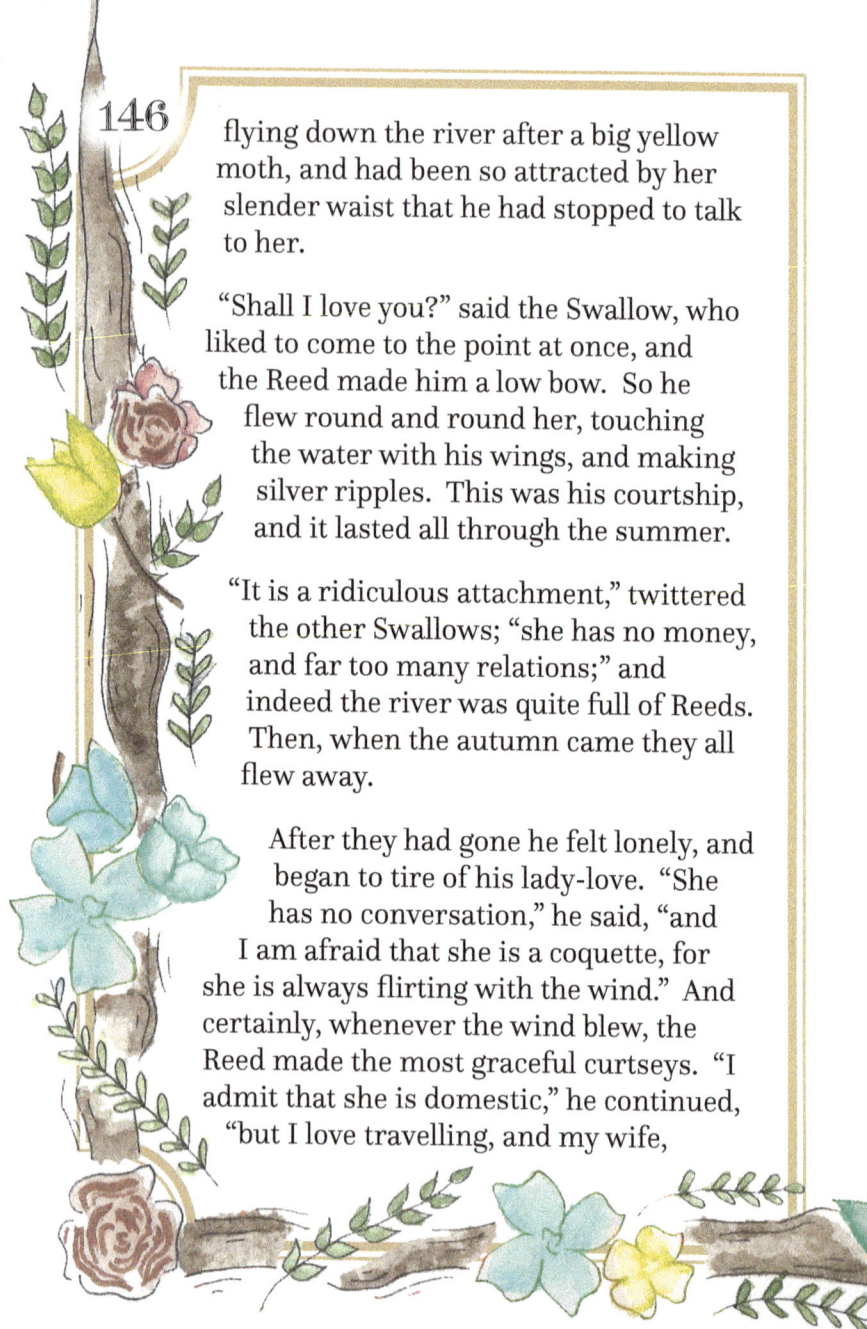

flying down the river after a big yellow moth, and had been so attracted by her slender waist that he had stopped to talk to her.

"Shall I love you?" said the Swallow, who liked to come to the point at once, and the Reed made him a low bow. So he flew round and round her, touching the water with his wings, and making silver ripples. This was his courtship, and it lasted all through the summer.

"It is a ridiculous attachment," twittered the other Swallows; "she has no money, and far too many relations;" and indeed the river was quite full of Reeds. Then, when the autumn came they all flew away.

After they had gone he felt lonely, and began to tire of his lady-love. "She has no conversation," he said, "and I am afraid that she is a coquette, for she is always flirting with the wind." And certainly, whenever the wind blew, the Reed made the most graceful curtseys. "I admit that she is domestic," he continued, "but I love travelling, and my wife, consequently, should love travelling also."

"Will you come away with me?" he said finally to her; but the Reed shook her head, she was so attached to her home.

"You have been trifling with me," he cried. "I am off to the Pyramids. Good-bye!" and he flew away.

All day long he flew, and at night-time he arrived at the city. "Where shall I put up?" he said; "I hope the town has made preparations."

Then he saw the statue on the tall column.

"I will put up there," he cried; "it is a fine position, with plenty of fresh air." So he alighted just between the feet of the Happy Prince.

"I have a golden bedroom," he said softly to himself as he looked round, and he prepared to go to sleep; but just as he was putting his head under his wing a large drop of water fell on him. "What a curious thing!" he cried; "there is not a single cloud in the sky, the stars are quite clear and bright, and yet it is raining. The climate in the north of Europe is really dreadful. The

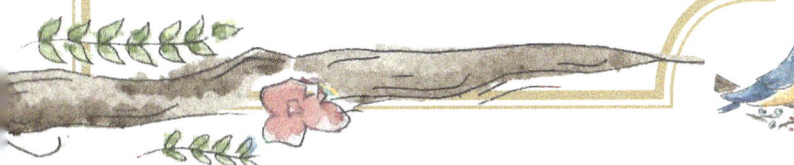

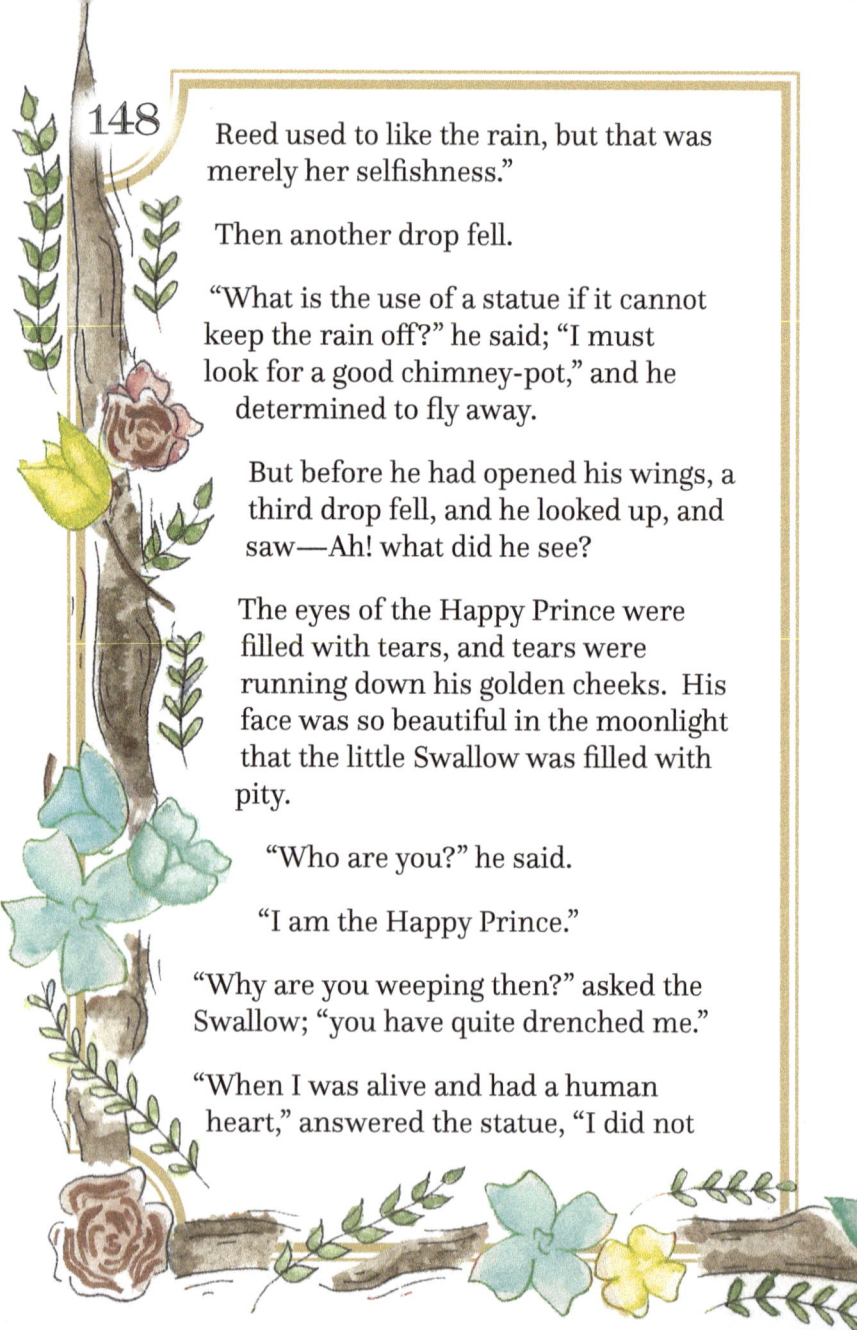

Reed used to like the rain, but that was merely her selfishness."

Then another drop fell.

"What is the use of a statue if it cannot keep the rain off?" he said; "I must look for a good chimney-pot," and he determined to fly away.

But before he had opened his wings, a third drop fell, and he looked up, and saw—Ah! what did he see?

The eyes of the Happy Prince were filled with tears, and tears were running down his golden cheeks. His face was so beautiful in the moonlight that the little Swallow was filled with pity.

"Who are you?" he said.

"I am the Happy Prince."

"Why are you weeping then?" asked the Swallow; "you have quite drenched me."

"When I was alive and had a human heart," answered the statue, "I did not know what tears were, for I lived in the Palace of Sans-Souci, where sorrow is not allowed to enter. In the daytime I played with my companions in the garden, and in the evening I led the dance in the Great Hall. Round the garden ran a very lofty wall, but I never cared to ask what lay beyond it, everything about me was so beautiful. My courtiers called me the Happy Prince, and happy indeed I was, if pleasure be happiness. So I lived, and so I died. And now that I am dead they have set me up here so high that I can see all the ugliness and all the misery of my city, and though my heart is made of lead yet I cannot chose but weep."

"What! is he not solid gold?" said the Swallow to himself. He was too polite to make any personal remarks out loud.

"Far away," continued the statue in a low musical voice, "far away in a little street there is a poor house. One of the windows is open, and through it I can see a woman seated at a table. Her face is thin and worn, and she has coarse, red hands, all pricked by the needle, for she is a seamstress. She is embroidering passion-flowers on a satin gown for the loveliest of the Queen's maids-of-honour to wear at the next Court-ball. In a bed in the corner of the room her little boy

is lying ill. He has a fever, and is asking for oranges. His mother has nothing to give him but river water, so he is crying. Swallow, Swallow, little Swallow, will you not bring her the ruby out of my sword-hilt? My feet are fastened to this pedestal and I cannot move."

"I am waited for in Egypt," said the Swallow. "My friends are flying up and down the Nile, and talking to the large lotus-flowers. Soon they will go to sleep in the tomb of the great King. The King is there himself in his painted coffin. He is wrapped in yellow linen, and embalmed with spices. Round his neck is a chain of pale green jade, and his hands are like withered leaves."

"Swallow, Swallow, little Swallow," said the Prince, "will you not stay with me for one night, and be my messenger? The boy is so thirsty, and the mother so sad."

"I don't think I like boys," answered the Swallow. "Last summer, when I was staying on the river, there were two rude boys, the miller's sons, who were always throwing stones at me. They never hit me, of course; we swallows fly far too well for that, and besides, I come of a family famous for its agility; but still, it was a mark of disrespect."

But the Happy Prince looked so sad that the little Swallow was sorry. "It is very cold here," he said; "but I will stay with you for one night, and be your messenger."

"Thank you, little Swallow," said the Prince.

So the Swallow picked out the great ruby from the Prince's sword, and flew away with it in his beak over the roofs of the town.

He passed by the cathedral tower, where the white marble angels were sculptured. He passed by the palace and heard the sound of dancing. A beautiful girl came out on the balcony with her lover. "How wonderful the stars are," he said to her, "and how wonderful is the power of love!"

"I hope my dress will be ready in time for the State-ball," she answered; "I have ordered passion-flowers to be embroidered on it; but the seamstresses are so lazy."

He passed over the river, and saw the

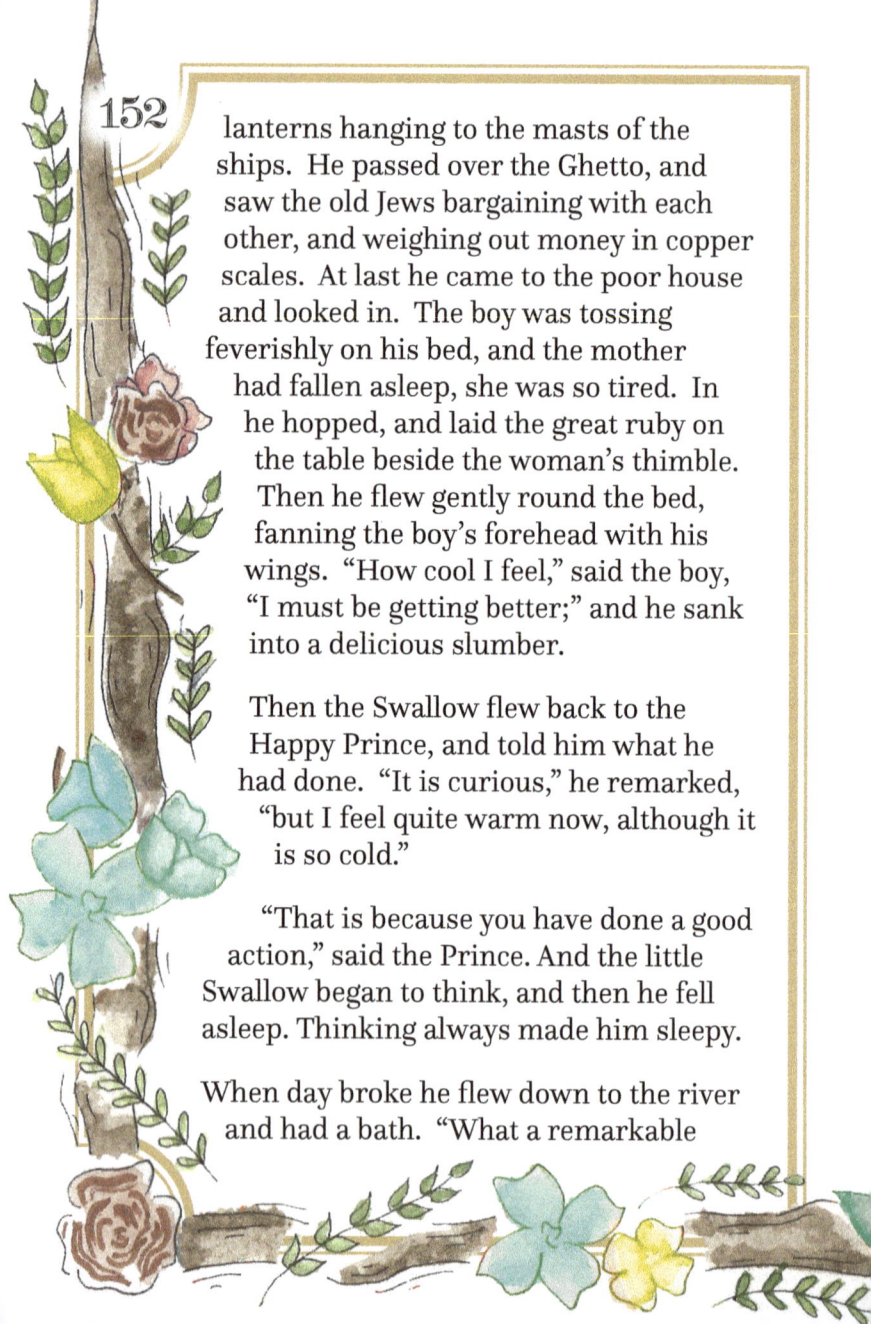

lanterns hanging to the masts of the ships. He passed over the Ghetto, and saw the old Jews bargaining with each other, and weighing out money in copper scales. At last he came to the poor house and looked in. The boy was tossing feverishly on his bed, and the mother had fallen asleep, she was so tired. In he hopped, and laid the great ruby on the table beside the woman's thimble. Then he flew gently round the bed, fanning the boy's forehead with his wings. "How cool I feel," said the boy, "I must be getting better;" and he sank into a delicious slumber.

Then the Swallow flew back to the Happy Prince, and told him what he had done. "It is curious," he remarked, "but I feel quite warm now, although it is so cold."

"That is because you have done a good action," said the Prince. And the little Swallow began to think, and then he fell asleep. Thinking always made him sleepy.

When day broke he flew down to the river and had a bath. "What a remarkable phenomenon," said the Professor of Ornithology as he was passing over the bridge. "A swallow in winter!" And he wrote a long letter about it to the local newspaper. Every one quoted it, it was full of so many words that they could not understand.

"To-night I go to Egypt," said the Swallow, and he was in high spirits at the prospect. He visited all the public monuments, and sat a long time on top of the church steeple. Wherever he went the Sparrows chirruped, and said to each other, "What a distinguished stranger!" so he enjoyed himself very much.

When the moon rose he flew back to the Happy Prince. "Have you any commissions for Egypt?" he cried; "I am just starting."

"Swallow, Swallow, little Swallow," said the Prince, "will you not stay with me one night longer?"

"I am waited for in Egypt," answered the Swallow. "To-morrow my friends will fly up to the Second Cataract. The river-horse couches there among the bulrushes, and on a great granite throne sits the God Memnon. All night long he watches the stars, and when the

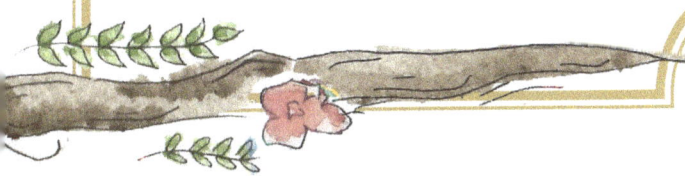

morning star shines he utters one cry of joy, and then he is silent. At noon the yellow lions come down to the water's edge to drink. They have eyes like green beryls, and their roar is louder than the roar of the cataract.

"Swallow, Swallow, little Swallow," said the Prince, "far away across the city I see a young man in a garret. He is leaning over a desk covered with papers, and in a tumbler by his side there is a bunch of withered violets. His hair is brown and crisp, and his lips are red as a pomegranate, and he has large and dreamy eyes. He is trying to finish a play for the Director of the Theatre, but he is too cold to write any more. There is no fire in the grate, and hunger has made him faint."

"I will wait with you one night longer," said the Swallow, who really had a good heart. "Shall I take him another ruby?"

"Alas! I have no ruby now," said the Prince; "my eyes are all that I have left. They are made of rare sapphires, which were brought out of India a thousand years ago. Pluck out one of them and take it to him. He will sell it to the jeweller, and buy food and firewood, and finish his play."

"Dear Prince," said the Swallow, "I cannot do that;" and he began to weep.

"Swallow, Swallow, little Swallow," said the Prince, "do as I command you."

So the Swallow plucked out the Prince's eye, and flew away to the student's garret. It was easy enough to get in, as there was a hole in the roof. Through this he darted, and came into the room. The young man had his head buried in his hands, so he did not hear the flutter of the bird's wings, and when he looked up he found the beautiful sapphire lying on the withered violets.

"I am beginning to be appreciated," he cried; "this is from some great admirer. Now I can finish my play," and he looked quite happy.

The next day the Swallow flew down to the harbour. He sat on the mast of a large vessel and watched the sailors hauling big chests out of the hold with ropes. "Heave a-hoy!" they shouted as each chest came up. "I am going to Egypt!"

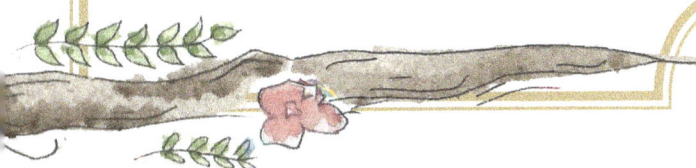

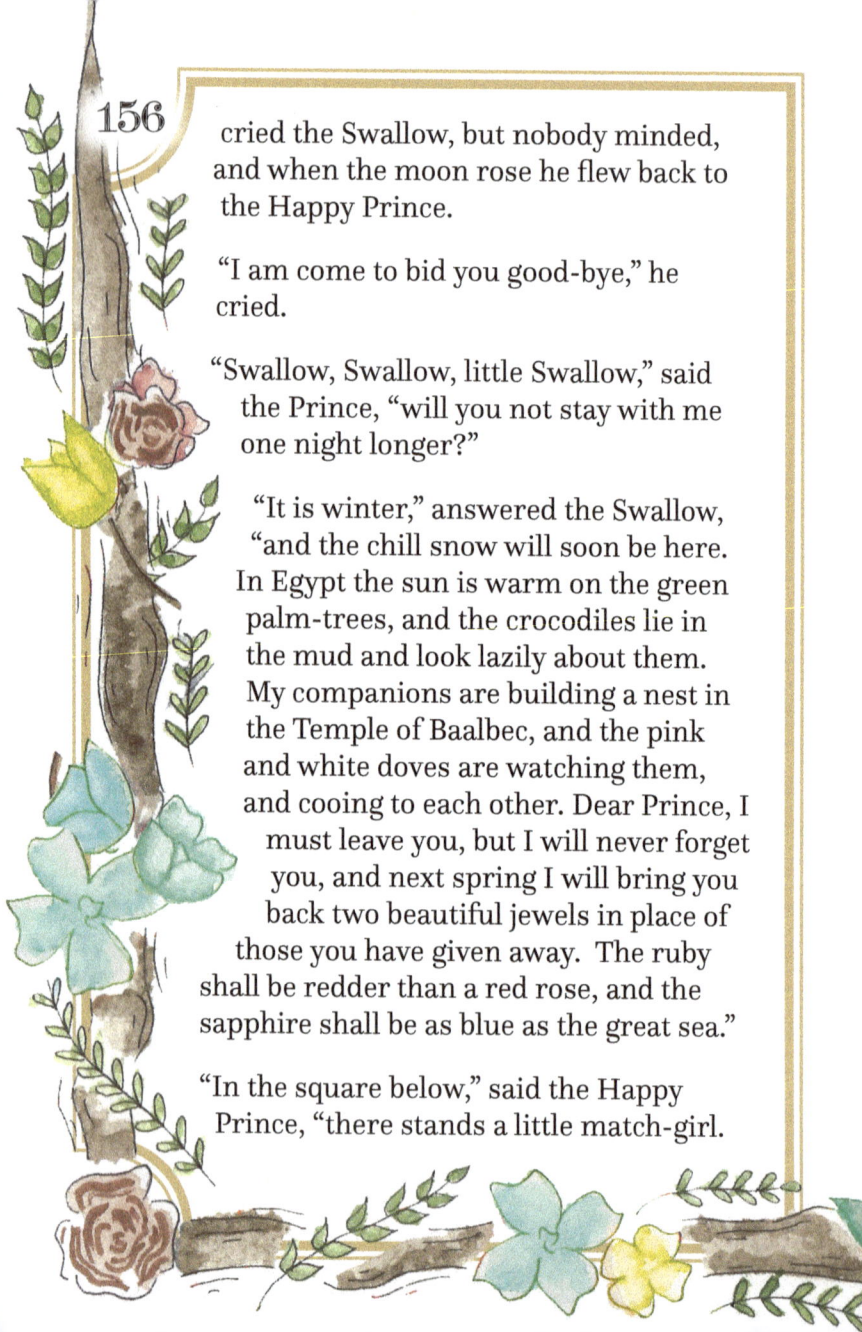

cried the Swallow, but nobody minded, and when the moon rose he flew back to the Happy Prince.

"I am come to bid you good-bye," he cried.

"Swallow, Swallow, little Swallow," said the Prince, "will you not stay with me one night longer?"

"It is winter," answered the Swallow, "and the chill snow will soon be here. In Egypt the sun is warm on the green palm-trees, and the crocodiles lie in the mud and look lazily about them. My companions are building a nest in the Temple of Baalbec, and the pink and white doves are watching them, and cooing to each other. Dear Prince, I must leave you, but I will never forget you, and next spring I will bring you back two beautiful jewels in place of those you have given away. The ruby shall be redder than a red rose, and the sapphire shall be as blue as the great sea."

"In the square below," said the Happy Prince, "there stands a little match-girl.

She has let her matches fall in the gutter, and they are all spoiled. Her father will beat her if she does not bring home some money, and she is crying. She has no shoes or stockings, and her little head is bare. Pluck out my other eye, and give it to her, and her father will not beat her."

"I will stay with you one night longer," said the Swallow, "but I cannot pluck out your eye. You would be quite blind then."

"Swallow, Swallow, little Swallow," said the Prince, "do as I command you."

So he plucked out the Prince's other eye, and darted down with it. He swooped past the match-girl, and slipped the jewel into the palm of her hand. "What a lovely bit of glass," cried the little girl; and she ran home, laughing.

Then the Swallow came back to the Prince. "You are blind now," he said, "so I will stay with you always."

"No, little Swallow," said the poor Prince, "you must go away to Egypt."

"I will stay with you always," said the Swallow, and he slept at the Prince's feet.

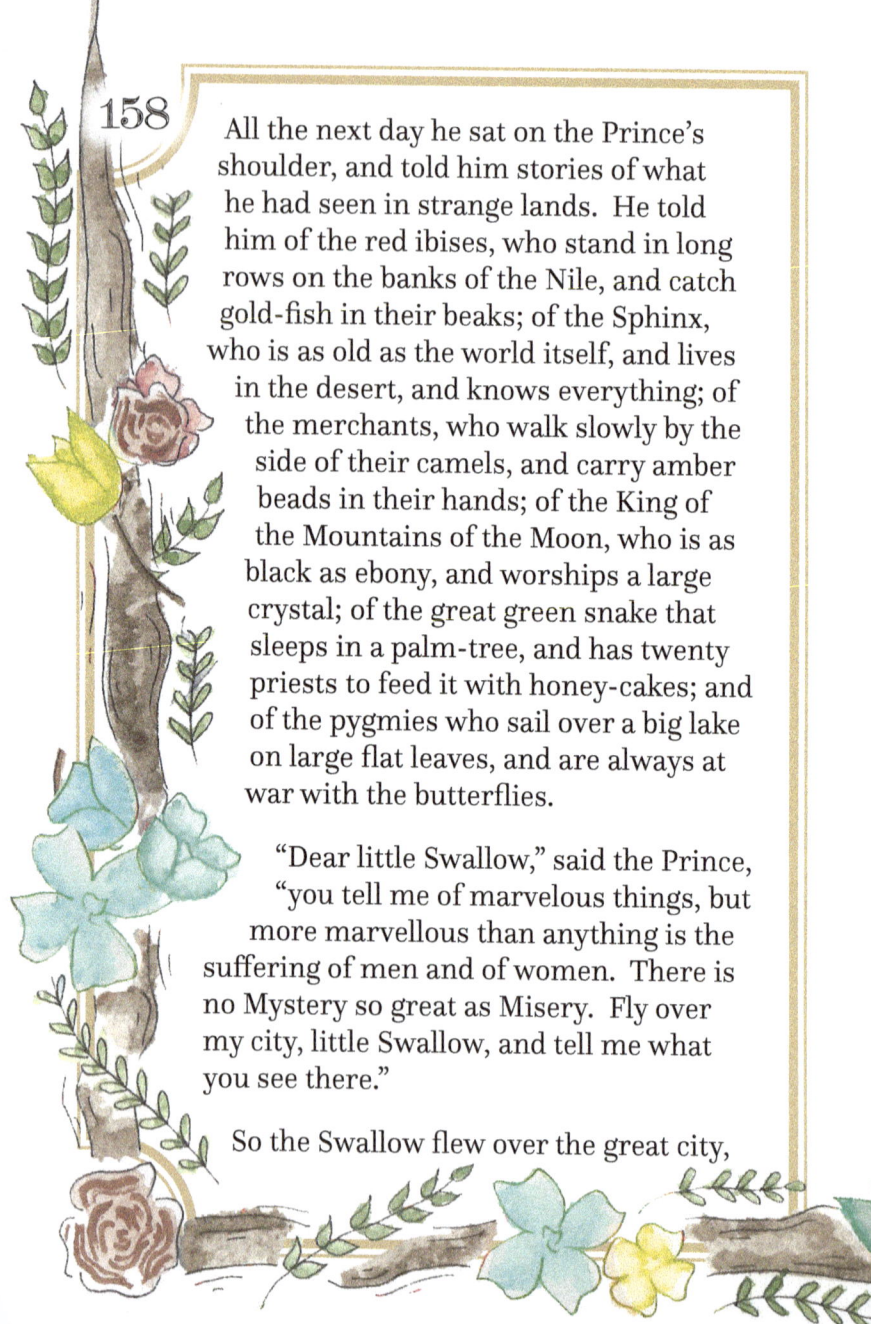

All the next day he sat on the Prince's shoulder, and told him stories of what he had seen in strange lands. He told him of the red ibises, who stand in long rows on the banks of the Nile, and catch gold-fish in their beaks; of the Sphinx, who is as old as the world itself, and lives in the desert, and knows everything; of the merchants, who walk slowly by the side of their camels, and carry amber beads in their hands; of the King of the Mountains of the Moon, who is as black as ebony, and worships a large crystal; of the great green snake that sleeps in a palm-tree, and has twenty priests to feed it with honey-cakes; and of the pygmies who sail over a big lake on large flat leaves, and are always at war with the butterflies.

"Dear little Swallow," said the Prince, "you tell me of marvelous things, but more marvellous than anything is the suffering of men and of women. There is no Mystery so great as Misery. Fly over my city, little Swallow, and tell me what you see there."

So the Swallow flew over the great city,

and saw the rich making merry in their beautiful houses, while the beggars were sitting at the gates. He flew into dark lanes, and saw the white faces of starving children looking out listlessly at the black streets. Under the archway of a bridge two little boys were lying in one another's arms to try and keep themselves warm. "How hungry we are!" they said. "You must not lie here," shouted the Watchman, and they wandered out into the rain.

Then he flew back and told the Prince what he had seen.

"I am covered with fine gold," said the Prince, "you must take it off, leaf by leaf, and give it to my poor; the living always think that gold can make them happy."

Leaf after leaf of the fine gold the Swallow picked off, till the Happy Prince looked quite dull and grey. Leaf after leaf of the fine gold he brought to the poor, and the children's faces grew rosier, and they laughed and played games in the street. "We have bread now!" they cried.

Then the snow came, and after the snow came the frost. The streets looked as if they were made of silver, they were so bright.

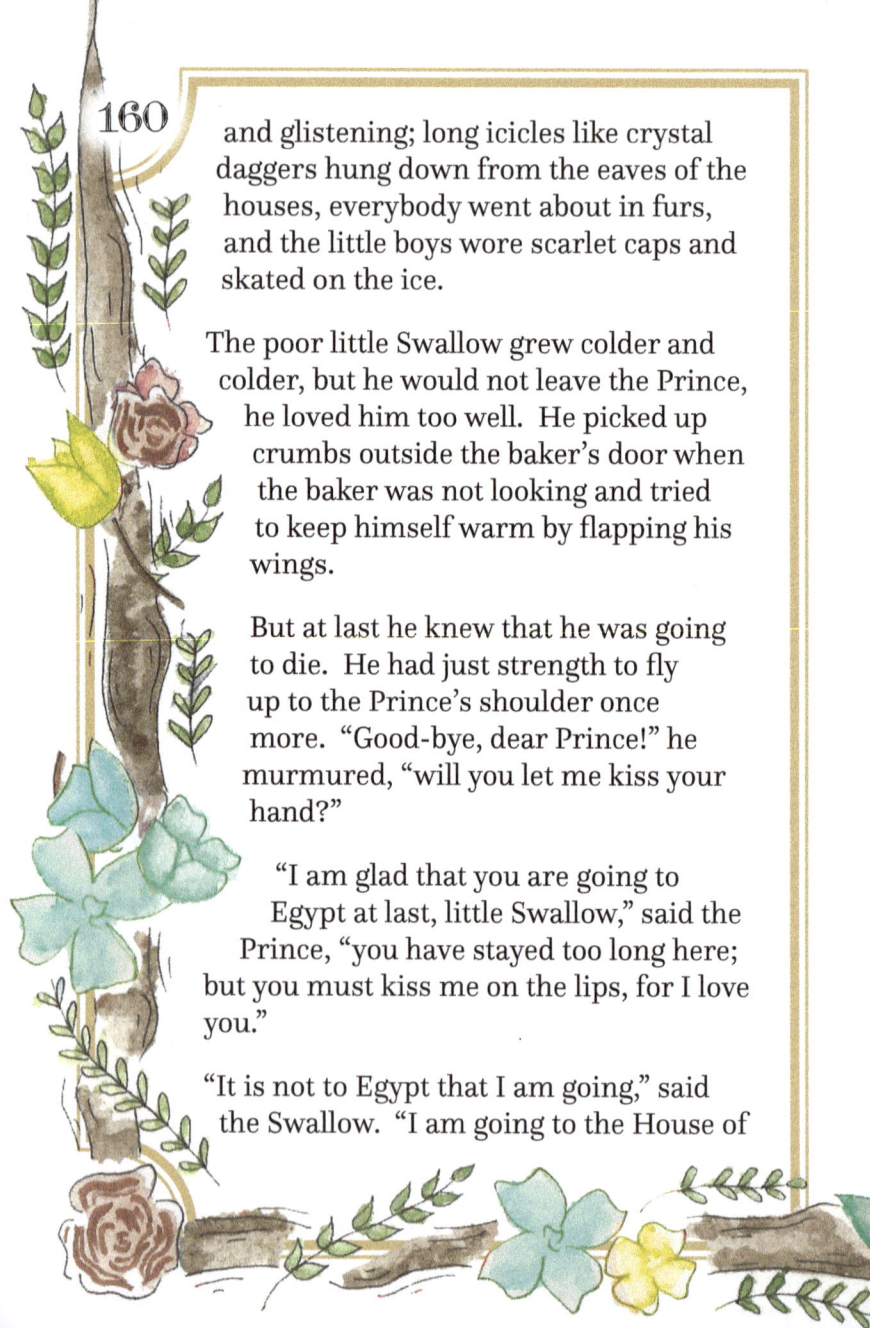

and glistening; long icicles like crystal daggers hung down from the eaves of the houses, everybody went about in furs, and the little boys wore scarlet caps and skated on the ice.

The poor little Swallow grew colder and colder, but he would not leave the Prince, he loved him too well. He picked up crumbs outside the baker's door when the baker was not looking and tried to keep himself warm by flapping his wings.

But at last he knew that he was going to die. He had just strength to fly up to the Prince's shoulder once more. "Good-bye, dear Prince!" he murmured, "will you let me kiss your hand?"

"I am glad that you are going to Egypt at last, little Swallow," said the Prince, "you have stayed too long here; but you must kiss me on the lips, for I love you."

"It is not to Egypt that I am going," said the Swallow. "I am going to the House of

Death. Death is the brother of Sleep, is he not?"

And he kissed the Happy Prince on the lips, and fell down dead at his feet.

At that moment a curious crack sounded inside the statue, as if something had broken. The fact is that the leaden heart had snapped right in two. It certainly was a dreadfully hard frost.

Early the next morning the Mayor was walking in the square below in company with the Town Councillors. As they passed the column he looked up at the statue: "Dear me! how shabby the Happy Prince looks!" he said.

"How shabby indeed!" cried the Town Councillors, who always agreed with the Mayor; and they went up to look at it.

"The ruby has fallen out of his sword, his eyes are gone, and he is golden no longer," said the Mayor in fact, "he is little better than a beggar!"

"Little better than a beggar," said the Town Councillors.

"And here is actually a dead bird at his feet!" continued the Mayor. "We must really issue

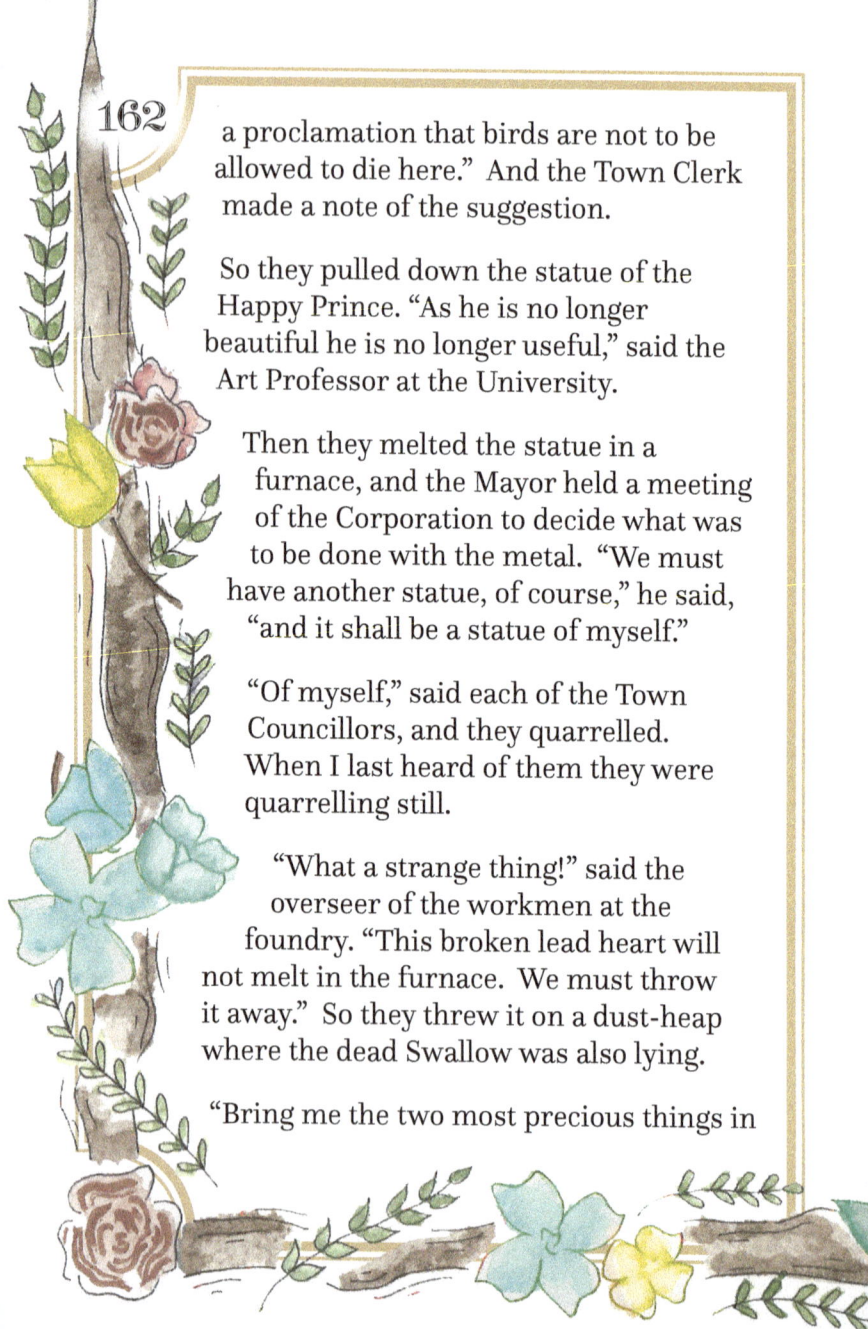

a proclamation that birds are not to be allowed to die here." And the Town Clerk made a note of the suggestion.

So they pulled down the statue of the Happy Prince. "As he is no longer beautiful he is no longer useful," said the Art Professor at the University.

Then they melted the statue in a furnace, and the Mayor held a meeting of the Corporation to decide what was to be done with the metal. "We must have another statue, of course," he said, "and it shall be a statue of myself."

"Of myself," said each of the Town Councillors, and they quarrelled. When I last heard of them they were quarrelling still.

"What a strange thing!" said the overseer of the workmen at the foundry. "This broken lead heart will not melt in the furnace. We must throw it away." So they threw it on a dust-heap where the dead Swallow was also lying.

"Bring me the two most precious things in

the city," said God to one of His Angels; and the Angel brought Him the leaden heart and the dead bird.

"You have rightly chosen," said God, "for in my garden of Paradise this little bird shall sing for evermore, and in my city of gold the Happy Prince shall praise me."

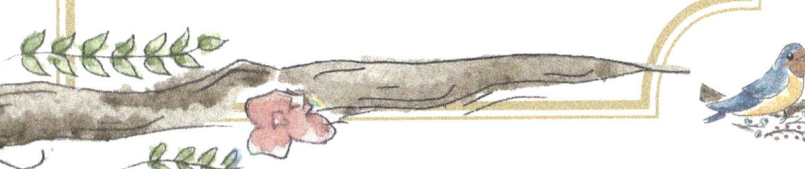

COMMENTS

Often in my youth, my mother read me "The Happy Prince" from a large hardcover I still own called *Tales of Princes and Princesses*. Despite the title, the story always made me sad. In Wilde's version, he adds his usual wit and humor, making the darkness of the tale a little lighter, but my melancholy remains.

My distinct memory as a child was that the prince had ignored the hardships of his people when alive. But that isn't so; rather, he was ignorant of them. And when he learns that life isn't as easy and pleasurable for the townspeople as it was for him during his life, he is saddened not only by this reality but also by the reality of his limitations to help them after his death.

The readers' lessons are many, but I've narrowed them down to three: 1) be aware of the lives just outside your normal world, and try your best to help them; 2) we aren't meant to function alone, even in helping other people; 3) self-sacrifice (of time, of material wealth, and even of our lives) is precious and will be rewarded. In the end, the prince is indeed happy—a happiness richer and fuller in death than ever it was in life.

Rehanna Mae '16

The Princess and the Pea

There once was a prince who wanted a bride,
but she had to be a *proper* princess,
delicate and true, outside and inside,
authenticated—the real deal. Distance
was no hindrance; he searched the whole mystic
world for a woman worth wedding. But he
found no one. This princess finding business
was lonely work. Then, one stormy night, beat-
ing at their castle door, was a soppy
sad sight who claimed to be a princess. "We'll
see," said the queen, who placed a single pea
under forty mattresses and beds. Real-
deal she was: she woke black, blue, and woeful,
but breakfast was toast and a proposal.

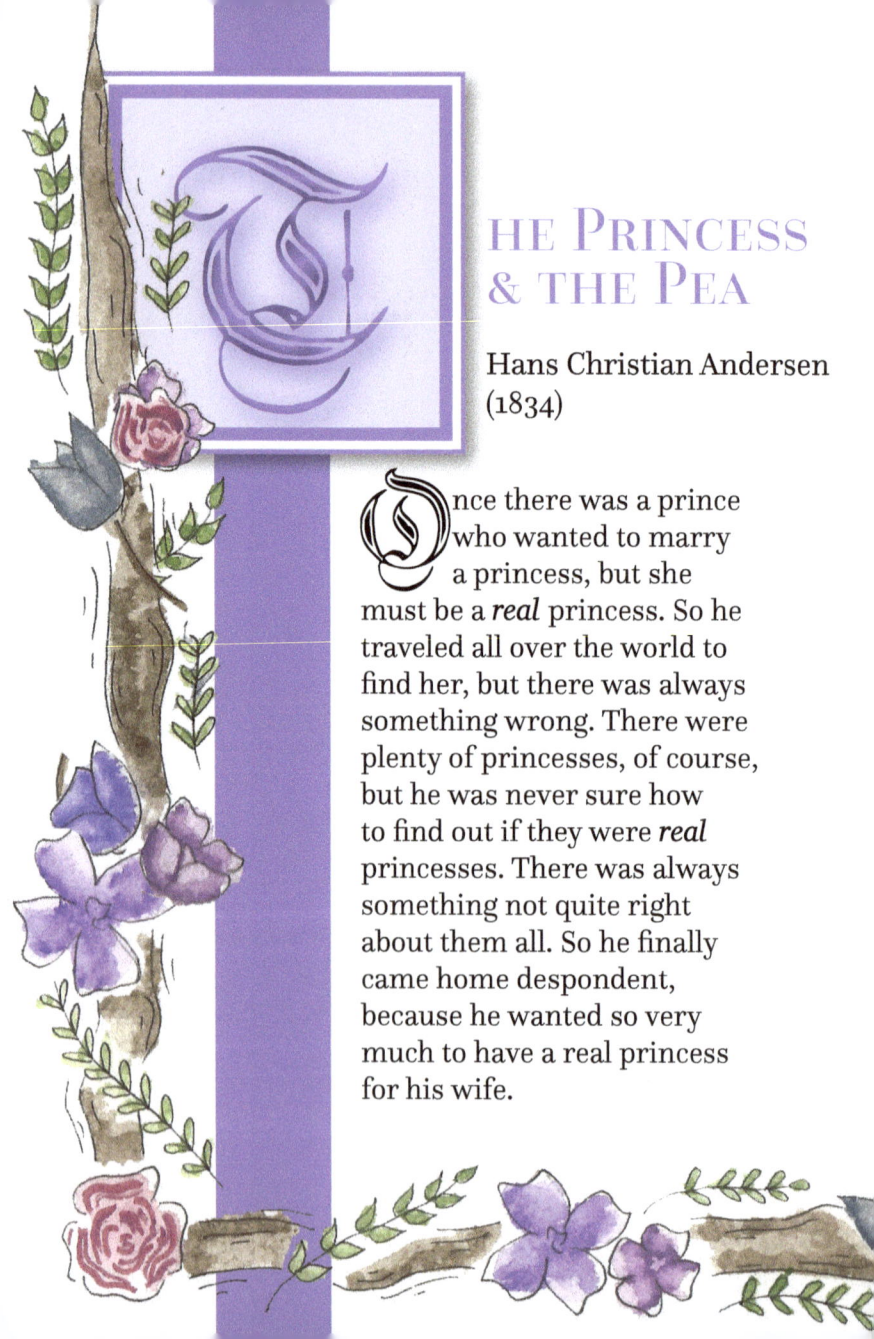

The Princess & the Pea

Hans Christian Andersen
(1834)

Once there was a prince who wanted to marry a princess, but she must be a *real* princess. So he traveled all over the world to find her, but there was always something wrong. There were plenty of princesses, of course, but he was never sure how to find out if they were *real* princesses. There was always something not quite right about them all. So he finally came home despondent, because he wanted so very much to have a real princess for his wife.

One evening there was a horrible storm. It thundered and lightened and rained. What a fearful night. Then there was a knock at the town gate, and the old king himself answered.

A princess stood there, water running down from her hair and clothes, into her shoes and out of the heels. Yet, despite her looking this way, she said she was a real princess.

"Well, we shall soon see about that," thought the old queen, who said nothing but went to prepare a bedroom for their guest. She striped away the blankets and sheets and placed a single pea on the bottom of the bed. Then she piled twenty mattresses on top of that pea, and another twenty feather beds on that. On top of all of this, the princess was to sleep that night.

The next morning, they asked her, "Did you sleep well?"

"Oh!" she said. "I barely slept at all. Goodness knows what was in that bed. It felt as though I was lying on something hard, and my entire body is black and blue this morning. It was dreadful."

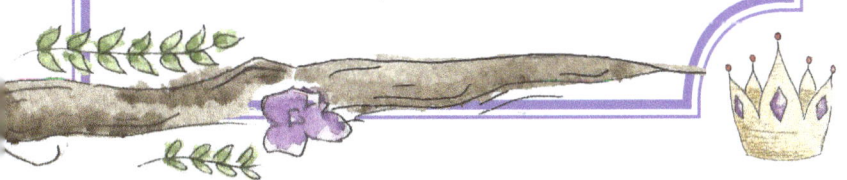

They knew at once she must be a real princess. Who else could be so delicate and sensitive as to feel a pea through twenty mattresses and twenty feather beds?

So the prince married her right away, for he was sure he had found a *real* princess indeed. And that pea was placed in a museum where it can still be seen today—unless someone stole it.

Now see, that was a real story!

Rendition by Jessa R. Sexton (2016)

COMMENTS

I love when the narrator makes some slight appearance in the tale, such as the Grimms' Hansel and Gretel ending with "my tale is done;" or Andersen's other story "Thumbelina," which explains the sparrow has given the story to the narrator; or the ending here: "Now see," he says directly to us, "that was a real story!" (Andersen). This is somewhat like breaking the fourth wall, which is when a character acknowledges the reader; both are an interesting way to connect with the audience.

In a similar Italian story from 1867, a prince is searching for "The Most Sensitive Woman," just as the tale is named. He keeps coming upon women who seem to be sad or suffering and feels a ray of hope he's found *the one*. But, after hearing each woman's story, he decides to continue his search, until he meets a woman crying over her bandaged foot because, she explains, a breeze blew a flower petal against her. Yes, seriously. And, yes, even more seriously, the prince tells her, "There cannot be a more sensitive woman than you," so he marries the girl (Schneller). Again the narrator speaks to us: "Did he do the right thing? Unfortunately the storyteller does not know, for she has run out of yarn" (Schneller).

Though humorous, I find this tale completely unsatisfying, and I'm rather grateful for Hans Christian Andersen's 1835 "The Princess and the Pea" which layers subtle humor with something far more fulfilling, and obviously longer-lasting. After reading this, women everywhere still pretend to have a poor night of sleep their first visit to the future in-laws, just in case Andersen is right, and that this is, in fact, "a real story!"

Rehanna Mae '16

The Maiden in the Tower

Rapunzel, Rapunzel, let down your hair
so I can climb this tower, which has no
stair. Your mother may have lost you to her
appetite, but I love you as my own,
my sweet delight. Rapunzel, Rapunzel,
let down your braid, so I can mount this wall
and have the maid whose rare song, round and full,
called me to such ardor that I, enthralled,
was led right then to wed her. Oh my only, Rapunzel, you've let down your guard, dear,
let's run to my kingdom, so our tales co-
here, and though your fairy godmum flies near
behind, though she may curse us, bear in mind,
she'll soon bless the love we'll build unconfined.

The Maiden in the Tower

Jessa R. Sexton (2016)

(inspired by Friedrich Schulz's 1790 version, with his wording in bold)

Once upon a time, because that's the best way to start off a story such as this, there were two young lovers who, despite the taunting and disapproval of their family, decided to get married. They were greatly in love and greatly happy—and happier still when they found out they were going to have a little baby.

They neighbored a fairy who spent most of her time and

all of her love on a beautiful garden
filled with manifold kinds of blossoms
and blooms, including an incredibly rare
flower called *Rapunzel*. The fairy had gathered
the seeds of this flower from far far far away,
and no one else in the entire land could boast of
having Rapunzels in her garden.

As the belly of the young pregnant wife grew, so
did her appetite, and one day she felt the distinct
and undeniable craving to eat Rapunzels.
Because she believed filling this craving would
be impossible, understanding that the fairy
never allowed anyone into her precious garden,
the young wife was grieved to the point that
she ceased eating entirely. Her husband grew
worried at his waning wife and asked her what
was wrong. **After she had hidden behind the
mountain**, as the old saying goes, for quite some
time, she finally told him of her craving for a
Rapunzel salad. At first the husband saw no way
to still her desire, **but because he held her very
dear, and because love overcomes all**, he spent
many days and nights walking around the fairy's
garden wall, trying to ascertain his entrance.

One lucky evening, he noticed the garden
door slightly ajar. He was quick about his
business of getting in

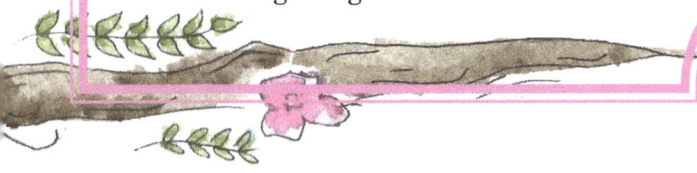

and gathering up Rapunzels in the most silent manner possible. How happy his wife was that night as she ate up that salad in **hot-hunger**. Except, the salad was so very tasty that her desire for more only grew grew grew. **(In those days Rapunzels still tasted gloriously.)**

Several nights in a row, the husband would return to the garden, but the gate was closed. Back home, his little wife again would eat nothing else and made herself thin and ill with longing. As young husbands do, the man felt he must do anything to please her, to take care of her. So when he finally saw the gate open again, he lept with joy and entered—only to find the fairy standing in his way of collecting more Rapunzels.

"What are you doing in my garden?" she asked.

Still shocked at having been caught, he didn't answer.

"You know no one is allowed in my garden. So why are you here?"

He fell to his knees in hope of forgiveness. "I apologize. I do! But I couldn't help it. My wife is wasting away from want. Nothing can satisfy her except Rapunzels, and your garden is the only one in the world with this rare flower. Please! You're a woman. Surely you can understand her pregnant cravings. She won't eat anything else. I just had to!"

The fairy did not understand, because, as much as she wanted a child of her own, she couldn't have one. But the situation suddenly steadied itself before her. "Oh? Well, fine. You can have all the Rapunzels you want. Give your dear wife what she needs. Don't let her waste away. I only ask for one thing in return."

"Anything!" he replied. "Anything at all for my love!"

"When your baby is born, you must bring her to me. She will be mine to raise as my own."

The husband was surprised at the request, but didn't see any way around it, so he accepted the fairy's terms. He was a little nervous explaining the deal to his wife, but she was out of her mind with her desire for the Rapunzels, and

because he answered that need, she loved him even more than she did before.

A few weeks after their baby girl was born, the couple received a visit from their fairy neighbor. With light and love in her eyes, the fairy approached the child, covered her in silver and gold fabrics, and sprinkled her with an enchanted water that blessed the baby with the grandest beauty in all the world.

"I shall call her *Rapunzel*," the fairy aptly named the child, whom she took home, raised carefully, and cherished dearly.

Considering herself Rapunzel's mother, and (quite obviously) caring for the child more than her actual parents did, the fairy began to worry about the safety of her beautiful girl. As Rapunzel grew older, the hazards of the world seemed to grow as well. So the fairy **conjured a high silver tower in the middle of a forest out of the earth**—with no door. One could enter only by a single window at the very top.

But don't feel too woeful for the teenaged Rapunzel. Her fairy-mum packed that sun-filled tower-top with **everything therein** to satisfy the girl's days with **glory and joy**. She had jewelry, dresses far better than any royalty could ever wish for, and a plethora of activities. Rapunzel could paint, knit, read, embroider, and sing, which became her favorite pastime of all. She had everything her heart could feasibly desire—except companionship.

Her fairy-mum visited her daily, bringing the finest meals imaginable and sharing a cup of tea and a chat. And though the young girl didn't remember anything different, something in her heart told her there *was* something different.

She would often times sit by the window, staring off into the forest and singing little tunes she wrote herself. They were a bit melancholy, as any teenager's song would be, and especially the song of a girl stuck alone in a tower. In the afternoons when the fairy-mum visited, she heard Rapunzel's sad songs, but the misguided fairy believed in her heart she was doing what was best to keep her lovely daughter safe.

One early afternoon, a young prince was hunting nearby, and he heard the

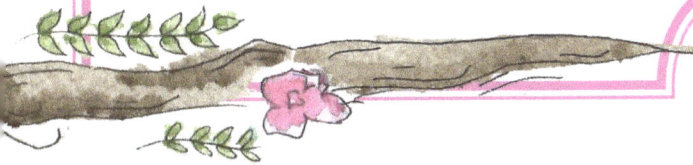

enchanting melody. Peering through some branches and squinting past the bright sunlight, the prince caught a glimpse of the face behind the alluring voice. Immediately, he loved her— because that's both acceptable and logical in a story such as this. But, search as he did, he couldn't figure out how the who to get into that tower. When he heard someone approaching, the prince darted back behind a tree. From there, he saw a beautiful fairy call out, "Rapunzel, Rapunzel, let down your hair, so I can climb this tower."

The prince watched as the longest braid of the loveliest golden hue tumbled out of the window, and up up up the fairy climbed. His plan was set— and all he had to do was wait wait wait until the fairy left.

It was late-afternoon when she finally climbed down. The prince waited until he knew she'd be far out of the forest before he approached the silver tower and, in his very best fairy voice, called out, "Rapunzel, Rapunzel, let down your hair, so I can climb this tower."

Rapunzel, used to her daily routine, was a little surprised at her fairy-mum's rapid return, but she was more-so grateful for the company, so she again dropped down her lovely tresses.

Ouch, she thought. *Why is my fairy-mum heavier? What on earth did she eat in that brief time she was away from me?*

And, because it was a rather high tower, she had even more time to ponder: *Oh! Maybe she's brought me a gift. Except I can't think of anything else I want. Really, though—she is pulling harder than usual this time.*

"I don't mean to be rude, but could you hurry it along? You're slower and rougher than usual..." she began to say out loud, but she was cut off by the sight of someone one hundred percent unexpected.

Rapunzel and the prince both found themselves word-less as they stared at each other: the prince because Rapunzel was even lovelier up close, and Rapunzel because the prince was not her fairy-mum. The silence was finally broken when the prince ran to and embraced Rapunzel, who was *not* prepared for or used to such affections.

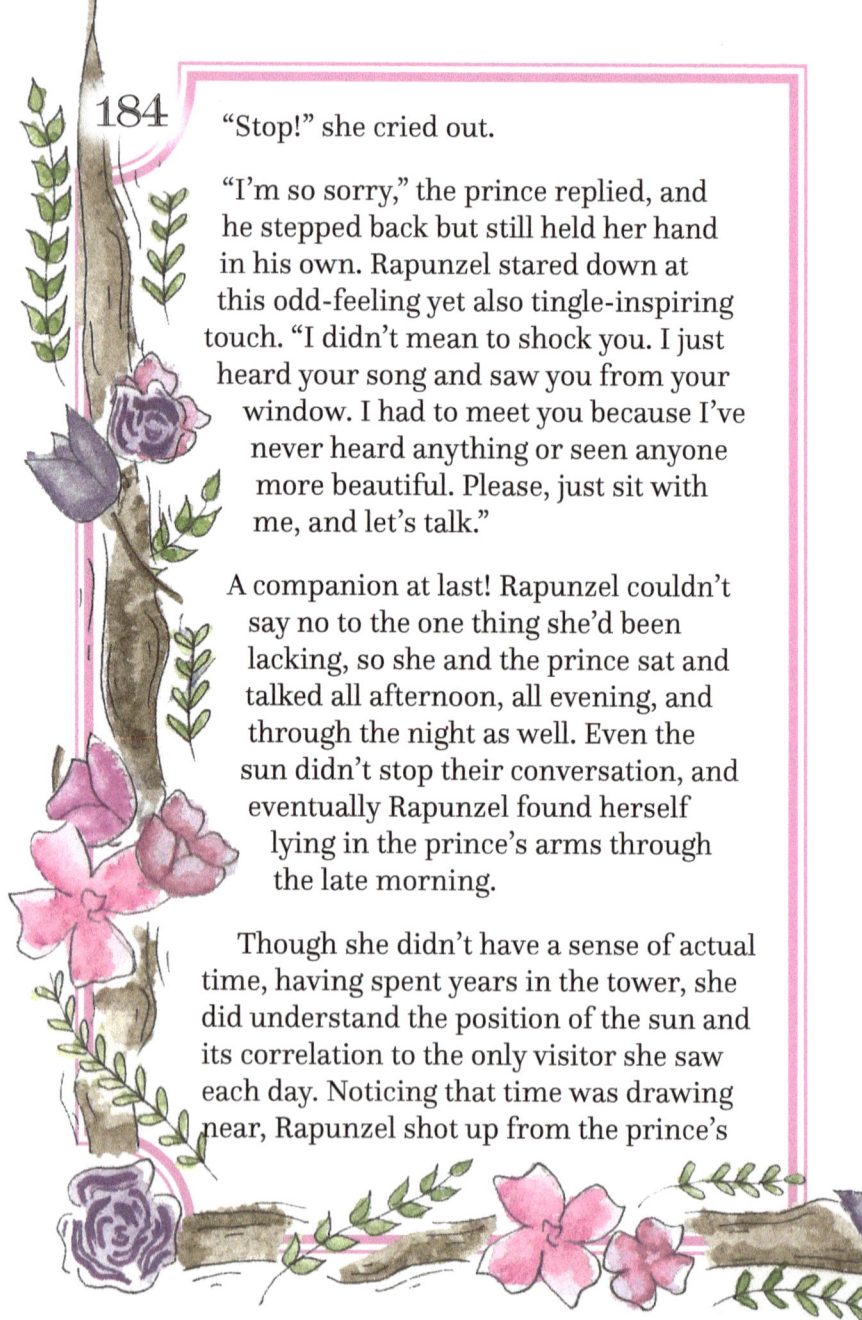

"Stop!" she cried out.

"I'm so sorry," the prince replied, and he stepped back but still held her hand in his own. Rapunzel stared down at this odd-feeling yet also tingle-inspiring touch. "I didn't mean to shock you. I just heard your song and saw you from your window. I had to meet you because I've never heard anything or seen anyone more beautiful. Please, just sit with me, and let's talk."

A companion at last! Rapunzel couldn't say no to the one thing she'd been lacking, so she and the prince sat and talked all afternoon, all evening, and through the night as well. Even the sun didn't stop their conversation, and eventually Rapunzel found herself lying in the prince's arms through the late morning.

Though she didn't have a sense of actual time, having spent years in the tower, she did understand the position of the sun and its correlation to the only visitor she saw each day. Noticing that time was drawing near, Rapunzel shot up from the prince's embrace and warned him that he had to depart.

"No, I never want to leave you!"

"Please—we'll both be in horrible trouble. You can...come back tomorrow. But you have to leave right now."

"No! I'm staying."

"What can I do to make you go?" Rapunzel offered in desperation.

The prince thought for barely a moment before he replied, "Marry me."

"What?"

"Be my wife. Right now. We'll perform the ceremony ourselves."

"That's crazy!"

"No. I love you. I knew it the moment I saw you. Marry me now, and I'll leave, only to return to my wife at nightfall."

Rapunzel was a little confused, but having so little interaction with others, having so enjoyed their time together, and still feeling the

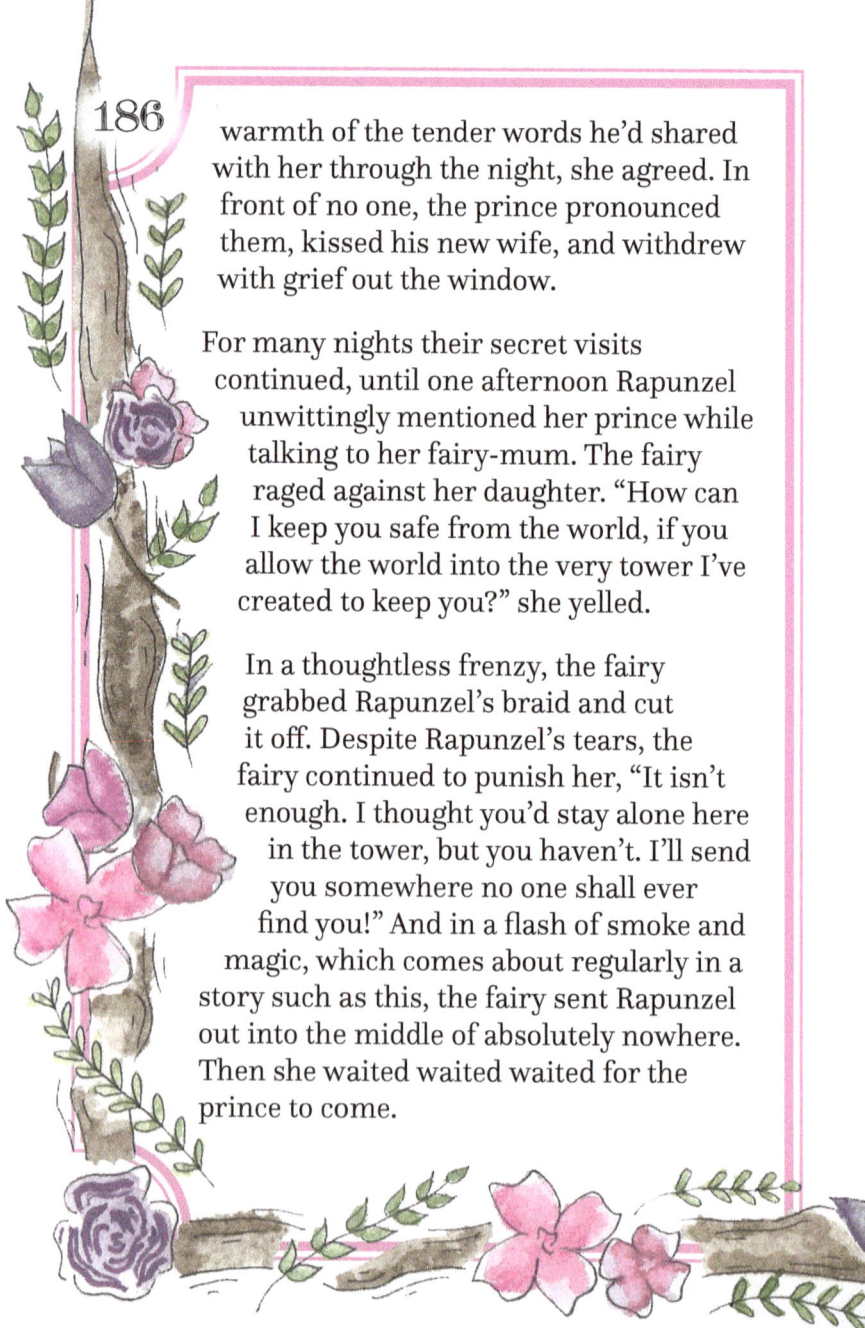

warmth of the tender words he'd shared with her through the night, she agreed. In front of no one, the prince pronounced them, kissed his new wife, and withdrew with grief out the window.

For many nights their secret visits continued, until one afternoon Rapunzel unwittingly mentioned her prince while talking to her fairy-mum. The fairy raged against her daughter. "How can I keep you safe from the world, if you allow the world into the very tower I've created to keep you?" she yelled.

In a thoughtless frenzy, the fairy grabbed Rapunzel's braid and cut it off. Despite Rapunzel's tears, the fairy continued to punish her, "It isn't enough. I thought you'd stay alone here in the tower, but you haven't. I'll send you somewhere no one shall ever find you!" And in a flash of smoke and magic, which comes about regularly in a story such as this, the fairy sent Rapunzel out into the middle of absolutely nowhere. Then she waited waited waited for the prince to come.

When he approached the window and called out to his wife, he was met, as always, by the long, blonde braid. As she steadied herself at the top of the tower, holding fast to the plait, the fairy thought to herself, *My goodness, how did my little Rapunzel every endure his climbing her hair?* And, because it was a very high tower, she had even more time to ponder: *perhaps love makes one stronger, better able to endure pain and waiting?* But that brief moment of insight and pity dissolved the instant she saw the shocked prince.

"Oh. Am I not the lady you were hoping to see?" she asked him.

"Where is Rapunzel? What have you done with her?" he yelled.

"She's nowhere. Literally. Nowhere. She broke my trust, and now I'll break you."

With that, the fairy threw the prince out of the tower. Somehow he didn't break his neck, perhaps because he fell in a thicket of rose bushes—but he did lose his eyesight from landing in the thorns. His eyes still worked for weeping, and he wandered wandered wandered

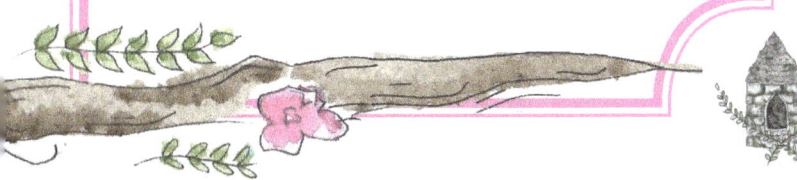

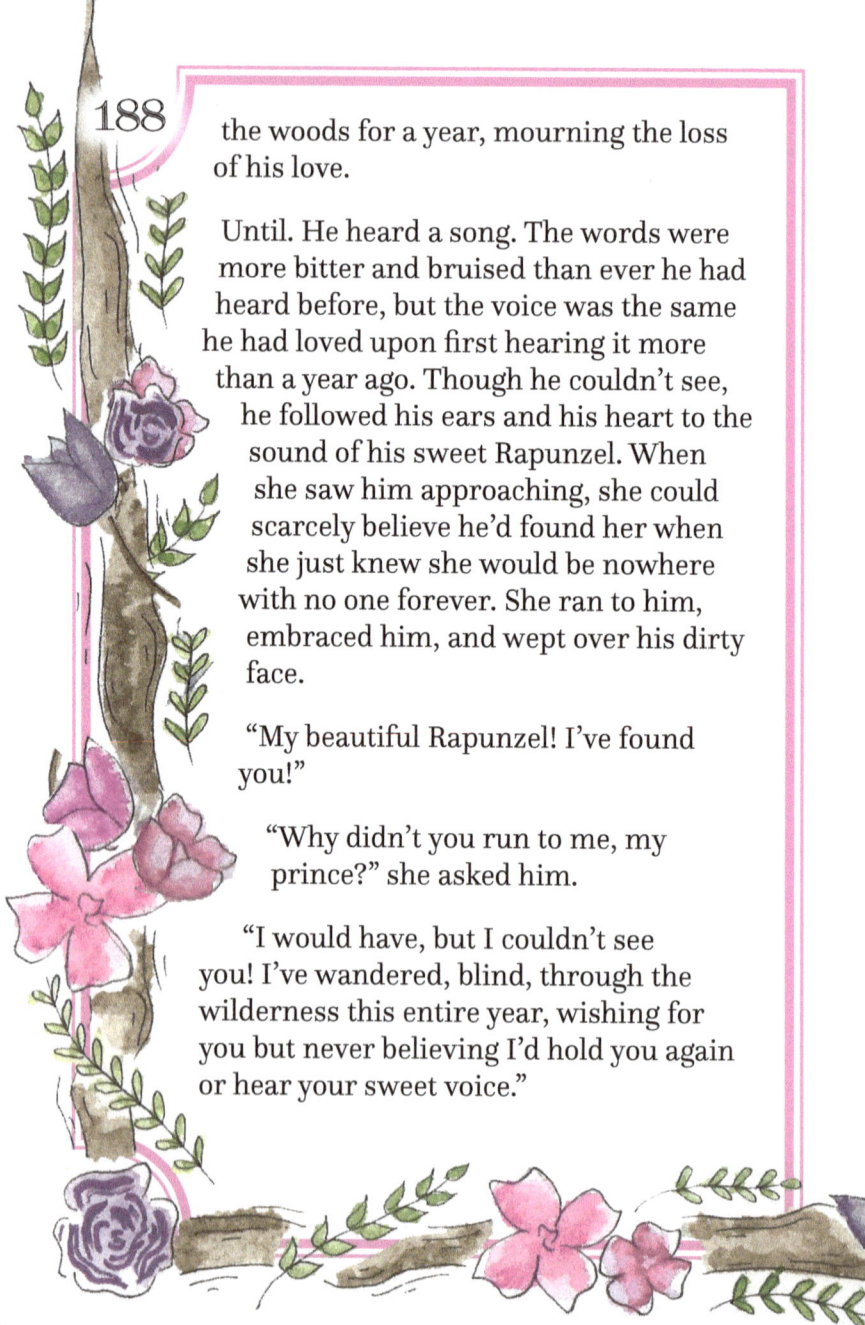

the woods for a year, mourning the loss of his love.

Until. He heard a song. The words were more bitter and bruised than ever he had heard before, but the voice was the same he had loved upon first hearing it more than a year ago. Though he couldn't see, he followed his ears and his heart to the sound of his sweet Rapunzel. When she saw him approaching, she could scarcely believe he'd found her when she just knew she would be nowhere with no one forever. She ran to him, embraced him, and wept over his dirty face.

"My beautiful Rapunzel! I've found you!"

"Why didn't you run to me, my prince?" she asked him.

"I would have, but I couldn't see you! I've wandered, blind, through the wilderness this entire year, wishing for you but never believing I'd hold you again or hear your sweet voice."

Rapunzel held his face close to hers, and, as she did, drops of her tears fell into his useless eyes, rendering them useful once again! (Don't ask how. This is a fairy tale.)

Blinking, he raised his head and looked at her once again. "My love! I can see you! Now everything is right again!"

Their joy was brief, though, as Rapunzel decided her thin prince needed a good meal. Having nothing much to do with herself the past year except sing and eat, she'd built herself a little wooden home and filled a corner with food from the forest. However, the fairy's curse followed them still, for every bit of food Rapunzel gave her love turned to stone. When she tried to eat a piece herself, the same horrible thing happened.

"Oh, my darling. We've found each other now, only to die of hunger," Rapunzel cried.

But they held each other fast.

"I don't care, Rapunzel. I'd rather die with you than live forever alone."

Remembering the sadness of her solitude, Rapunzel agreed with her husband's sweet words. And the two of them tried to

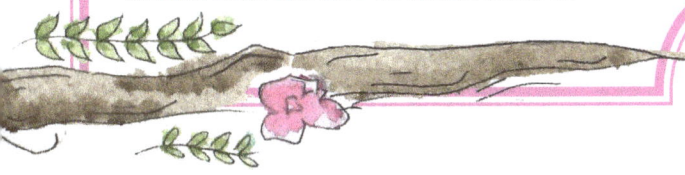

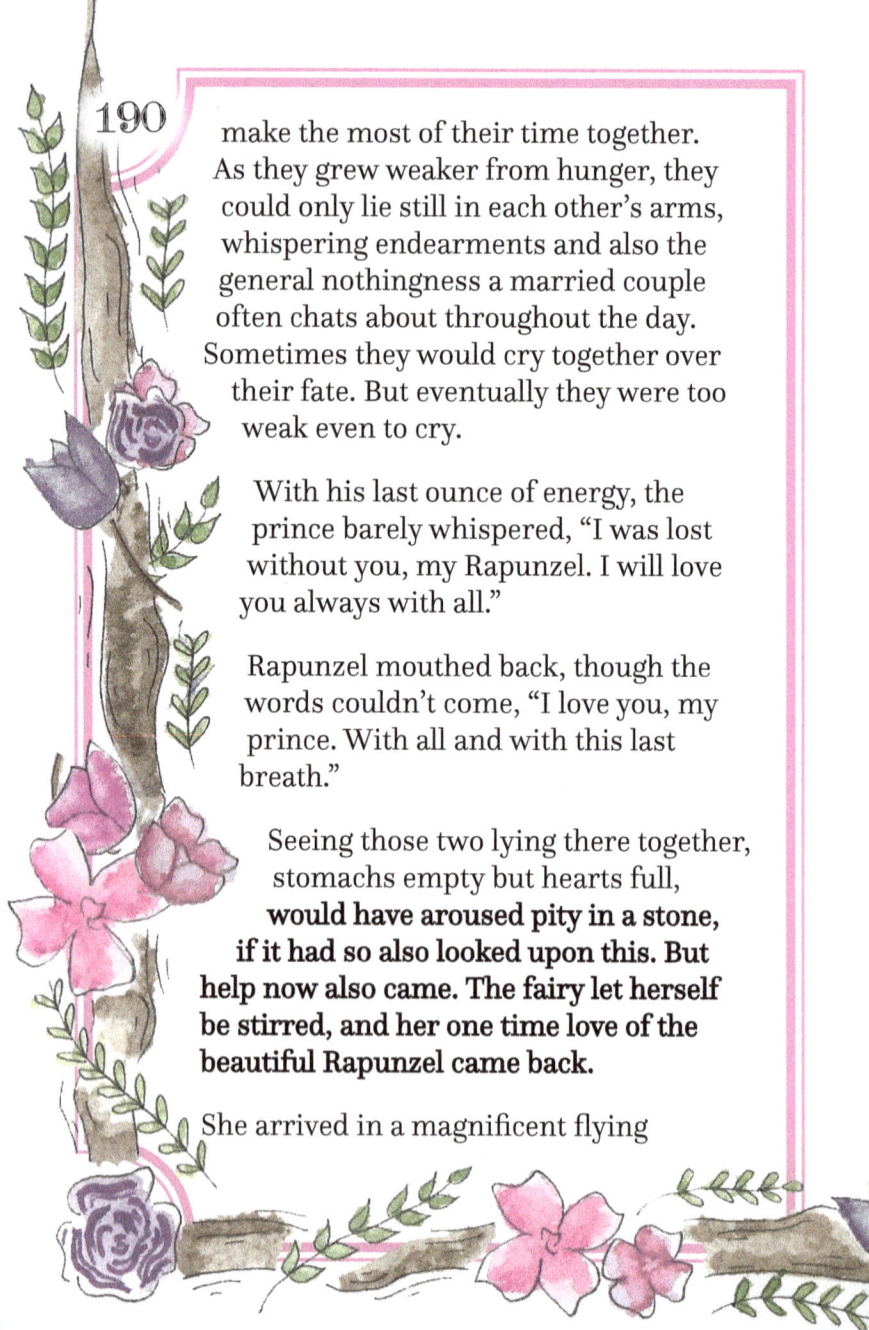

make the most of their time together. As they grew weaker from hunger, they could only lie still in each other's arms, whispering endearments and also the general nothingness a married couple often chats about throughout the day. Sometimes they would cry together over their fate. But eventually they were too weak even to cry.

With his last ounce of energy, the prince barely whispered, "I was lost without you, my Rapunzel. I will love you always with all."

Rapunzel mouthed back, though the words couldn't come, "I love you, my prince. With all and with this last breath."

Seeing those two lying there together, stomachs empty but hearts full, **would have aroused pity in a stone, if it had so also looked upon this. But help now also came. The fairy let herself be stirred, and her one time love of the beautiful Rapunzel came back.**

She arrived in a magnificent flying

carriage, and just in time too. She scooped up the near-lifeless couple and laid them gently on a blanket of the finest fabrics and flew them to the palace of the prince. The king's heart was overwhelmed with joy, as he'd nearly completely lost all hope his dear son would return. And this joy was doubled, as the son had returned with a wife. When the prince and Rapunzel were well again, they would still spend the evenings lying next to each other in a warm embrace, sometimes whispering far through the night.

"My beautiful Rapunzel," the prince would say, even into their old age, "I was truly lost without you. I will love you always with all."

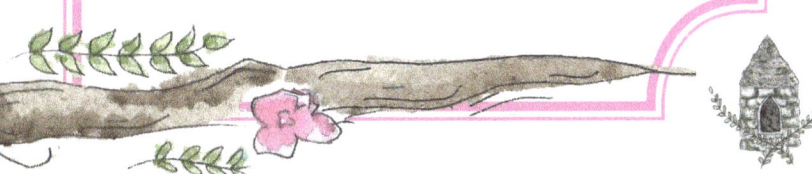

Comments

The story of the long-haired maiden in the tower has a myriad of variations. The Italian "Parsley" of about 1634 deals with an ogress and a mother craving parsley. The mother herself is caught stealing the ogress's parsley and must give away her daughter or die for her sins.

Italy's "The Fairy Angolia" of 1870 incorporates a witch, the more commonly-used antagonist in this fairy tale. Again a pregnant woman is caught stealing from a garden, this time jujubes, and again her penance is giving up her daughter. Angolia is eight before the witch claims her. In this story, the prince who climbs her hair runs away with Angolia. They are chased by the witch, who throws magic balls of yarn at them. Though they survive this attack, the witch curses Angolia with a dog face. "How can I take you to you home to my parents?" the prince asks. "They would never allow me to marry a maiden with a dog's face." Yes. I laughed here. I don't apologize. In the end it is her own pet dog that pleads her case to the witch, who lifts the curse. The prince then feels confident in taking Angolia home, and they have a lovely wedding.

Pineau's French "Blond Beauty" from

1891 echoes the ugly curse theme when the fairy punishes Blond Beauty for escaping the "castle without doors" by turning her into a frog. In the end, this fairy does reverse the curse and helps Blond Beauty and her prince win a large portion of the king's kingdom.

The French "Persinette" ends with the woman (who is not called a fairy but has two sisters who are fairies) finding out from her goddaughter's blabbering pet parrot that Persinette has had a male visitor in her tower. (Angolia is fortunate to have a faithful pup instead.) When the couple tries to escape, the woman takes away Persinette's beauty and kills the young man. Persinette returns to her godmother and later marries another prince. This story isn't romantic at all. I can see how it didn't quite catch on.

My favorite version is Friedrich Schulz's 1790 tale. I decided to write my own, however, for a couple of reasons. One is because I wanted to try my hand at fairy-tale writing. Another is because Schulz's story is quite racy. Both he and the Grimm brothers write of Rapunzel having a secret wedding ceremony and then becoming pregnant in the tower. And though the Grimm version is more well-known, I wanted to base my writing on Schulz's mainly because I love the fairy character, who truly does love Rapunzel, over the Grimm witch/sorceress. Even though Schulz's fairy continues to curse Rapunzel and the prince after they are reunited despite all odds, in the end her love overcomes her anger, and she carries the couple to the palace. I did leave out the entire portion about Rapunzel having twins. I wanted to simplify the story, keeping it about two lovers who were lost without each other, literally and romantically.

'16 Rehema Mae

Silver-Hair &
Those Three Bears

One day Silver-Hair, searching for blooms or
butterflies, wandered unwittingly far
into the forest and smack in front of
the snug residence of three absent bears.

Who wouldn't enter that part-opened door?
Who wouldn't taste test a porridge snack bar,
or try out three different-sized seats, or love
to nap in a stranger's wee bed upstairs?

Well, Silver-Hair did all these things and snoozed
soundly through the first questions of growling
Big-bear, calm Middle-bear, and piped-voice Little bear: "Somebody ate our food, abused
our chairs, and tumbled our beds!" Then prowling
Silver woke—and ran as fast as legs get!

ILVER-HAIR

& the Three Bears

Joseph Cundall (1849)

In a far-off country there was once a little girl who was called Silver-hair, because her curly hair shone brightly. She was a sad romp, and so restless that she could not be kept quiet at home, but must needs run out and away, without leave.

One day she started off into a wood to gather wild flowers, and into the fields to chase butterflies. She ran here and she ran there, and went so far, at last, that she found herself in a lonely place, where she saw a snug little house, in

which three bears lived; but they were
not then at home.

The door was ajar, and Silver-hair pushed it
open and found the place to be quite empty, so
she made up her mind to go in boldly, and look
all about the place, little thinking what sort of
people lived there.

Now the three bears had gone out to walk a
little before this. They were the Big Bear, and
the Middle-sized Bear, and the Little Bear; but
they had left their porridge on the table to cool.
So when Silver-hair came into the kitchen, she
saw the three bowls of porridge. She tasted the
largest bowl, which belonged to the Big Bear, and
found it too cold; then she tasted the middle-
sized bowl, which belonged to the Middle-sized
Bear, and found it too hot; then she tasted the
smallest bowl, which belonged to the Little Bear,
and it was just right, and she ate it all.

She went into the parlour, and there were
three chairs. She tried the biggest chair, which
belonged to the Big Bear, and found it too high;
then she tried the middle-sized chair, which
belonged to the Middle-sized Bear, and she found
it too broad; then she tried the little chair, which
belonged to the Little Bear, and found it just

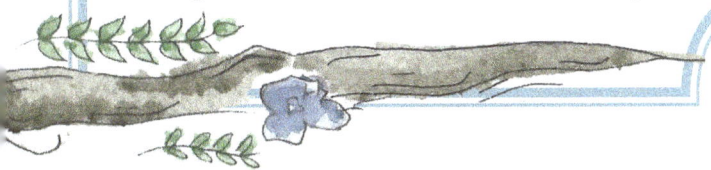

right, but she sat in it so hard that she broke it.

Now Silver-hair was by this time very tired, and she went upstairs to the chamber, and there she found three beds. She tried the largest bed, which belonged to the Big Bear, and found it too soft; then she tried the middle-sized bed, which belonged to the Middle-sized Bear, and she found it too hard; then she tried the smallest bed, which belonged to the Little Bear, and she found it just right, so she lay down upon it, and fell fast asleep.

While Silver-hair was lying fast asleep, the three bears came home from their walk. They came into the kitchen, to get their porridge, but when the Big Bear went to his, he growled out:

"SOMEBODY HAS BEEN TASTING MY PORRIDGE!"

and the Middle-sized Bear looked into his bowl and said:

"Somebody Has Been Tasting My Porridge!"

and the Little Bear piped:

"Somebody has tasted my porridge and eaten it all up!"

Then they went into the parlour, and the Big Bear growled:

"SOMEBODY HAS BEEN SITTING IN MY CHAIR!"

and the Middle-sized Bear said:

"Somebody Has Been Sitting In My Chair!"

and the Little Bear piped:

"Somebody has been sitting in my chair, and has broken it all to pieces!"

So they went upstairs into the chamber, and the Big Bear growled:

"SOMEBODY HAS BEEN TUMBLING MY BED!"

and the Middle-sized Bear said:

"Somebody Has Been Tumbling My Bed!"

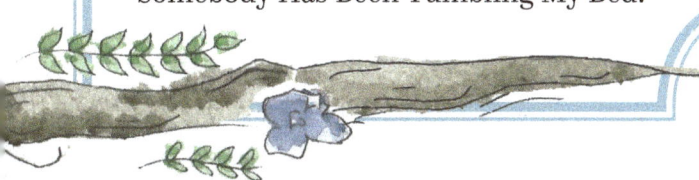

and the Little Bear piped:

"Somebody has been tumbling my bed, and here she is!"

At that, Silver-hair woke in a fright, and jumped out of the window and ran away as fast as her legs could carry her, and never went near the Three Bears' snug little house again.

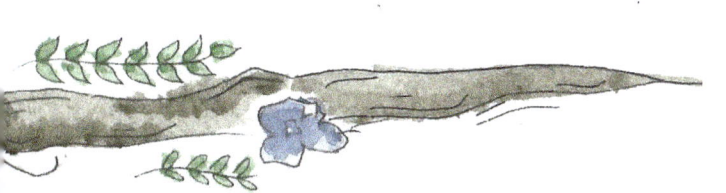

COMMENTS

The story of "Goldilocks and the Three Bears" is one of the most-retold I know, and the retellings these days range from *Goldilocks and the Three Dinosaurs* (by one of my favorite authors Mo Willems) to *Goldilocks and Just One Bear* (by Leigh Hodgkinson) in which Baby Bear is all grown up and finds himself lost in the city, wandering into a nice loft apartment and messing up the home goods of none other than the now-grown Goldilocks who once did the same to him in his little cabin in the woods.

As far as the evolution of the common and most well-known version by Mother Goose (who made the bears a family), the earlier story lines have some interesting variations. Eleanor Mure's 1813 handwritten tale speaks of an old woman who breaks into the home of three bears "because they snubbed her during a recent social call." The ending is quite violent as the bears try different methods to kill her.

Robert Southey's version is one of my favorites. This tale also has an old woman who peeps into the bears' house and then lets herself in. "If she had been a good little old

Woman," Southey writes, "she would have waited till the Bears came home, and then, perhaps, they would have asked her to breakfast; for they were good Bears—a little rough or so, as the manner of Bears is, but for all that very good natured and hospitable. But she was an impudent, bad old Woman" (11) who ends up saying "wicked words" when the porridge doesn't suit her and when she breaks the littlest chair (12). The end of this version just explains her fate is unknown after she jumps out of the window and runs off.

Even though I love Southey's humor, I did want to work with a version that had a little girl instead of an old woman. That cut out John Batten's story of three bears and a fox but opened the door of Joseph Cundall's story, shared above. I prefer it to Flora Annie Steel's "The Story of the Three Bears" from 1904—the first to call the protagonist *Goldilocks*—though the progression of the name went from

- Cundall's Silver-hair in 1849 to
- Silverlocks in 1858 to
- Golden Hair in 1868 to
- Little Golden-Hair in 1889

before Steel's granting her the name that has kept with her forever after (*Goldilocks and the Three Bears: Special Edition*). Unlike Silver-hair (who is portrayed as restless, curious, and blithe), Goldilocks is an "impudent, rude little girl" reminiscent of the old woman Southey describes (Steel).

Besides, I wanted to challenge our common recollection of this character's name and her hair color—and to see what magic illustrator Rehanna could concoct with her paints and pencils for our "Silver-hair" lead.

'16 Rehman Mae

Sleeping Beauty

Grow, Beauty, and with these fairy gifts become a princess full of goodness and grace,
joy and gentleness, with a lovely face
and a royal heart of sweetness and glee.

Hide, Beauty, from the darkening decree,
a coveting curse: the evil embrace
of stagnation—of lost life through the space
of forever as you slumber and breathe.

Sleep, Beauty, and in that sleep may restful
dreams attend your every whim and need. May
you escape the wrath and ever-vengeful
pride of the one who will look in dismay

when I end the altered curse with gentle
kisses—turning your ever-night to Day.

LITTLE BRIER-ROSE

Jacob & Wilhelm Grimm (1812)

Long ago a king and a queen greatly wanted children, but they had none. One day the queen was bathing, and a little frog hopped out of the water and towards her and said, "Your wish for a child will soon come true: you will have a little daughter." And so it happened.

The king was so delighted by the birth of Princess Rose that he held a merry celebration. He wanted to invite the thirteen fairies who lived in his kingdom. But because fairies had to be served on golden plates, and the palace had only twelve, one fairy was left out.

At the end of the festivities, each fairy presented the baby with a gift. One blessed her with virtue, one with grace, one with joy, one with gentleness, one with beauty, one with sweetness, and so on. The twelfth fairy was about to present her gift when the thirteenth fairy arrived. Offended by the lack of invitation, she cursed the child: "In her fifteenth year, the princess will prink her finger with a spindle and fall over dead."

When she vanished, the twelfth fairy approached to calm the horrified parents. "I cannot remove the curse, but my gift is to alter it. She will not die. She will only sleep for a hundred years." Still, the king hoped to save his daughter by issuing an order to destroy all spindles in the kingdom.

The princess became older and more beautiful through the years. One day, not far into her fifteenth year, her parents went away on a trip. Rose wandered through the castle, exploring spaces she hadn't before. Eventually she came to an old tower. She found a narrow staircase and followed her curiosity up until she reached

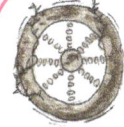

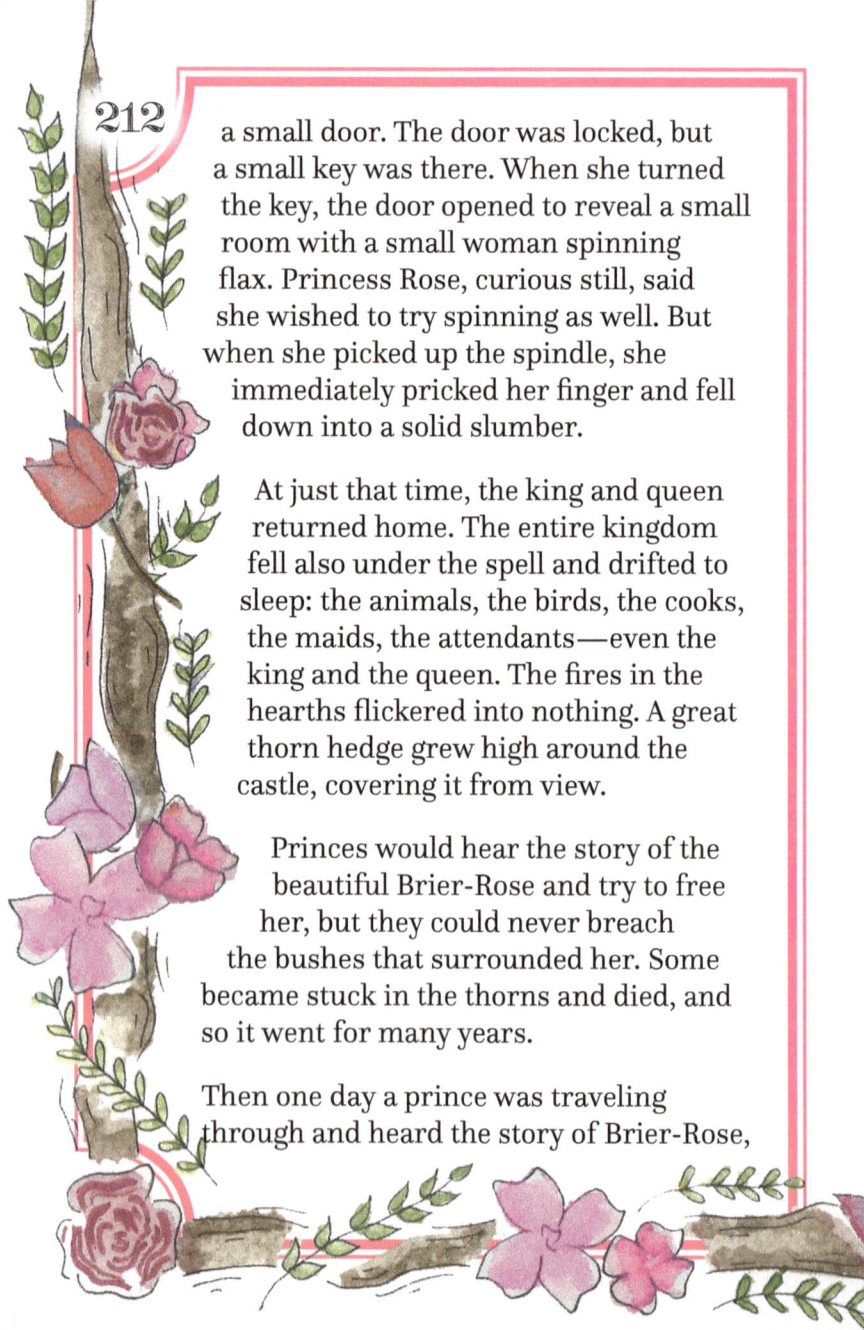

a small door. The door was locked, but a small key was there. When she turned the key, the door opened to reveal a small room with a small woman spinning flax. Princess Rose, curious still, said she wished to try spinning as well. But when she picked up the spindle, she immediately pricked her finger and fell down into a solid slumber.

At just that time, the king and queen returned home. The entire kingdom fell also under the spell and drifted to sleep: the animals, the birds, the cooks, the maids, the attendants—even the king and the queen. The fires in the hearths flickered into nothing. A great thorn hedge grew high around the castle, covering it from view.

Princes would hear the story of the beautiful Brier-Rose and try to free her, but they could never breach the bushes that surrounded her. Some became stuck in the thorns and died, and so it went for many years.

Then one day a prince was traveling through and heard the story of Brier-Rose, now almost a legend some thought to be true while others weren't so sure— the story of the beautiful princess asleep, surrounded by all in her kingdom; the details of the other princes who tried to save her and died in the thorns.

"I have no fear of thorns," he said. "I will be the one to free the Rose from the briers."

And so he went boldly forth, but when he approached the thorns, they turned to flowers. The hedge separated for him, creating a path, but as he passed through, the path behind him closed up, and the flowers turned back into thorns. Once inside the courtyard, he saw the animals asleep on the ground and the birds asleep on the roof. He walked into the castle and saw the cooks and the maids and the attendants—even the king and the queen— sleeping.

Finally he saw the old tower and walked the same stairway the princess had many many years ago. When he saw Brier-Rose, he was so overcome by her beauty that he couldn't help but to kiss her. Immediately, she awoke. And so did the animals and the birds and the cooks and the maids and the attendants—even the king

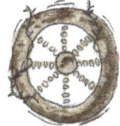

and the queen. The fires in the hearth roared once again.

So the prince and Princess Brier-Rose were married, and they lived a long and happy life together.

Rendition by Jessa R. Sexton (2016)

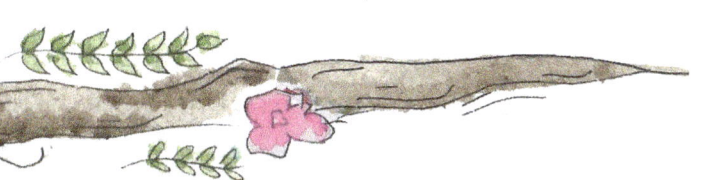

COMMENTS

"'The Sleeping Beauty' is best known today in two different versions: Perrault's, and that of the Brothers Grimm" (Bettleheim 227). Indeed, I went back and forth on which of these to share. Perrault writes in 1697 that the old fairy who curses the princess isn't invited to the party because everyone figures she is dead, as no one has heard from her in fifty years. The Grimm tale of 1812 has the king and queen unable to invite all thirteen of the fairies of the land because fairies have to eat from golden plates, and the castle has only twelve of these. Both versions could have avoided all problems if only the royalty had better etiquette. Disney's latest version, *Maleficent*, which shows a completely different view of the so-considered evil fairy, explains she curses the baby in part because she was once lovers with the king, who hideously betrayed her. Though this story doesn't follow the classic design, it provides an interesting twist worth exploring—and by that I mean you should watch the film.

Another large difference between the two most popular versions is the sleeping and waking of the princess and her court. In

Perrault's tale, the court is put to sleep by the good fairy who altered the curse of death, as the fairy worries the princess will wake up confused if her surroundings have changed too much. Her parents, however, do not sleep; they decree for the castle to be left alone, but they leave, grow old, and die; so the land is eventually ruled by another king. From that royal line comes the prince who rescues Sleeping Beauty, who wakes when he enters her room—sans kiss! Here a huge change takes place, as Perrault's story continues on with an entirely dissimilar second half about the prince having an ogress as a mother, and the challenges this brings the newly wedded beauty and her savior prince.

In the end I chose the Grimm version, titled "Little Brier Rose," because it has the entire court (her parents included) falling asleep and subsequently waking up when she does. And what wakes her? The classic kiss by the prince. He doesn't know that will break the spell; he is simply drawn to kiss the beautiful sleeping girl. The realist in me has always wondered about hundred-year-old-nap-breath. The romantic in me says that a fairy who can alter the curse of death surely also altered the curse of malodor.

Afterword:
A Note on Sonnets

The most famous sonneteer was William Shakespeare. You've probably heard of him. I find his sonnet form the easiest to write.

All sonnets have fourteen lines, each line with ten syllables.

This ten syllable line is said to have iambic pentameter. (An iam means two syllables; pent means five; two times five equals ten, so the meter is ten syllables!)

The three most popular sonnet form rhyme schemes and the fairy tale sonnets that follow that form are listed below:

Italian

a b b a   a b b a

The remaining six lines are called a sestet and can have either two or three rhyming sounds, arranged in a variety of ways:

c d c d c d
c d d c d c
c d e c d e

c d e c e d
c d c e d c
c d c d e e

("Sleeping Beauty," "Hansel and Gretel," "Cinderella")

Spenserian

a b a b b c b c c d c d e e

Shakespearean

a b a b c d c d e f e f g g

("The Maiden in the Tower," "The Princess and the Pea," "The Happy Prince," "Thumbelina," "The Mermaid," "Little Red Riding Hood," "Pyramus and Thisbe," "Snow White")

And I, hoping to one day be a famous Sonneteer as well, created my own form, whose name I am still playing around with.

Hilliardian

abcd abcd efgefg

("Silver-Hair and Those Three Bears")

Bibliography

Andersen, Hans Christian. "The Princess and the Pea." Trans. E. V. Lucas and H.B. Paull. *Andersen's Fairy Tales*. New York: Grosset & Dunlap, 1963. Print. 274-75.

—. "The Princess and the Peas." *Victorian Fairy Tales*. Ed. Michael Newton. Oxford: Oxford University Press, 2015. Print. 6-7.

—. "Thumbelina." *Hans Andersen Forty-Two Stories*.Trans. M.R. James. 1930. London: Faber and Faber, 1953. Project Gutenberg eBook.

—. "Thumbelina." *The Yellow Fairy Book*. Ed. Andrew Lang. London: The Folio Society, 2010. Print. 313-24.

Basile, Giambattista. "Parsley (Petrosinella)." *Rapunzel and Other Folktales*. Ed. D. L. Ashliman. 29 December 2015. Web. 2008-2015.

Batten, John. "Scrapefoot (An English Tale)." *Goldilocks and the Three Bears: Special Edition*. USA: Enhanced Ebooks Publishing, 2014. Kindle.

Bettelheim, Bruno. *The Uses of Enchantment: The Meaning and Importance of Fairy Tales*. New York: Vintage Books, 2010. Print.

Blair, Elizabeth. "Why Are Old Women Often the Face of Evil in Fairy Tales and Folklore?" *NPR.org*. 11 November 2015. Web. 28 October 2015.

Cundall, Joseph. "Silver-hair and the Three Bears." *Goldilocks and the Three Bears: Special Edition*. Ed. Damian Stevenson. USA: Enhanced Ebooks Publishing, 2014. Kindle.

"The Fair Angiola." *Rapunzel and Other Folktales*. Ed. D. L. Ashliman. 29 December 2015. Web. 2008-2015.

Fansler, Dean S. "Juan and Clotilde (Philippines)." *Rapunzel and Other Folktales.* Ed. D. L. Ashliman. 29 December 2015. Web. 2008-2015.

"The Grandmother (France)." *Little Red Riding Hood and Other Tales.* Ed. D. L. Ashliman. Collected by Achille Millien. Translated by D. L. Ashliman. 25 January 2015. Web. 2008-2015.

Grimm, Jacob and Wilhelm. "Cinderella." *Fairy Tales for Home and Nursery.* Trans. Margaret Hunt. Germanstories.vcu. edu. 24 Feb. 2016. Web. 2014.

—. "Cinderella." *Grimms' Fairy Tales.* Trans. E.V. Lucas, Lucy Crane, and Marian Edwardes. New York: Grosset & Dunlap, 1963. Print. 148-56.

—. "Hansel and Gretel." *Fairy Tales for Home and Nursery.* Trans. Margaret Hunt. Germanstories.vcu.edu. 24 Feb. 2016. Web. 2014.

—. "Hansel and Gretel." *Grimms' Fairy Tales.* Trans. E.V. Lucas, Lucy Crane, and Marian Edwardes. New York: Grosset & Dunlap, 1963. Print. 238-47.

—. "Briar Rose (Sleeping Beauty)." *Grimms' Fairy Tales.* Trans. E.V. Lucas, Lucy Crane, and Marian Edwardes. New York: Grosset & Dunlap, 1963. Print. 96-100.

—. "Rapunzel." *Grimms' Fairy Tales.* Trans. E.V. Lucas, Lucy Crane, and Marian Edwardes. New York: Grosset & Dunlap, 1963. Print. 124-28.

—. "Red Riding Hood." *Grimms' Fairy Tales.* Trans. E.V. Lucas, Lucy Crane, and Marian Edwardes. New York: Grosset & Dunlap, 1963. Print. 224-28.

—. "Snow White." *Fairy Tales for Home and Nursery.* Trans. Margaret Hunt. Germanstories.vcu.edu. 24 Feb. 2016. Web. 2014.

—. "Snow-White and the Seven Dwarfs." *Grimms' Fairy Tales.* Trans. E.V. Lucas, Lucy Crane, and Marian Edwardes. New York: Grosset & Dunlap, 1963. Print. 157-68.

Hamilton, Edith. "Pyramus and Thisbe." *Mythology: Timeless Tales of Gods and Heroes*. New York: Grand Central Publishing, 2011. Print.

Hans Christian Andersen's Thumbelina. Dir. Don Bluth and Gary Goldman. Perf. Jodi Benson, Gary Imhoff, Carol Channing, John Hurt, Charo, and Gilbert Gottfried. 20th Century Fox, 1994. DVD.

"The Happy Prince." *Tales of Princes and Princesses*. New York: Exeter Books, 1987. Print. 4-10.

Lang, Andrew. "Prunella (Italy)." *Rapunzel and Other Folktales*. Ed. D. L. Ashliman. 29 December 2015. Web. 2008-2015.

—. "The Three Bears." *Goldilocks and the Three Bears: Special Edition*. Ed. Damian Stevenson. USA: Enhanced Ebooks Publishing, 2014. Kindle.

"Little Red Hat (Italy/Austria)." *Little Red Riding Hood and Other Tales*. Ed. D. L. Ashliman. Translated by D. L. Ashliman. 25 January 2015. Web. 2008-2015.

"Little Red Hood (Lower Lusatia)." *Little Red Riding Hood and Other Tales*. Ed. D. L. Ashliman. Translated by A. H. Wratislaw. 25 January 2015. Web. 2008-2015.

"Little Red Hood." *Sixty Folk-Tales from Exclusively Slavonic Sources*. Trans. A. H. Wratislaw. 1890. *Sacredtexts.com*. 24 Feb. 2016. Web. n.d.

Maleficent. Dir. Robert Stromberg. Perf. Angelina Jolie, Sharlto Copley, and Elle Fanning. Walt Disney Pictures, 2014. DVD.

"The Many Versions of Cinderella: One of the Most Ancient Fairy Tales." *Swide.com*. 11 November 2015. Web. 21 February 2015.

Maurel, Josephine. "Parsillette (France)." *Rapunzel and Other Folktales*. Ed. D. L. Ashliman. Translated by D.L. Ashliman. 29 December 2015. Web. 2008-2015.

"The Mermaid of Edam." *Tales Told in Holland.* Ed. Olive Beaupre Miller. Chicago: The Book House for Children, 1926. Print. 18-22.

"Mermaid." *Occultopedia.com.* n.d. Web. 17 February 2015.

Nicol, George. "The Story of the Three Bears." *Goldilocks and the Three Bears: Special Edition.* Ed. Damian Stevenson. USA: Enhanced Ebooks Publishing, 2014. Kindle.

Perrault, Charles. "Little Red Riding Hood (France)." *The Blue Fairy Book.* Ed. Andrew Lang. London: The Folio Society, 2010. Print. 51-53.

—. "The Sleeping Beauty in the Wood." *The Blue Fairy Book.* Ed. Andrew Lang. London: The Folio Society, 2010. Print. 54-63.

Pineau, Leon. "La Belle Blonde (France)." *Rapunzel and Other Folktales.* Ed. D. L. Ashliman. Translated by D. L. Ashliman. 29 December 2015. Web. 2008-2015.

"The Princess and the Pea." *Tales of Princes and Princesses.* New York: Exeter Books, 1987. Print. 20-23.

Schneller, Christian. "The Most Sensitive Woman (Italy)." Ed. D. L. Ashliman. Translated by D. L. Ashliman. 27 January 2015. Web. 2008-2015.

Schulz, Friedrich. "Rapunzel (1790)." *A New Translation of the 1790 Tale by Friedrich Schulz.* Translated by Oliver Loo. 2015. Kindle.

"Sleeping Beauty." *Tales of Princes and Princesses.* New York: Exeter Books, 1987. Print. 24-30.

Snow White and The Huntsman. Dir. Rupert Sanders. Perf. Charlize Theron, Kristen Stewart, and Chris Hemsworth. Universal Pictures, 2012. Amazon Prime.

Southey, Robert. "The Three Bears." *Goldilocks and the Three Bears: Special Edition.* Ed. Damian Stevenson. USA: Enhanced Ebooks Publishing, 2014. Kindle.

Steel, Flora Annie. "The Story of the Three Bears." *Goldilocks and the Three Bears: Special Edition*. Ed. Damian Stevenson. USA: Enhanced Ebooks Publishing, 2014. Kindle.

Wilde, Oscar. "The Happy Prince." *Complete Fairy Tales of Oscar Wilde*. New York: Signet Classic, 1990. Print. 5-10.

—. "'The Happy Prince' by Oscar Wilde read by Stephen Fry FULL UNABRIDGED." Gareth Roberts. *Youtube.com*. 23 February 2016. Web. 24 May 2013.

If you enjoyed this book, check out its companion!

Little Stories of Enchantment
TWELVE FAIRY TALE SONNETS
FOR CHILDREN

JESSA R. SEXTON   REHANNA MAE GRANT

www.hilliardinstitute.com

ABOUT THE ILLUSTRATOR

Rehanna Mae Grant is a fashion designer and artist from Tennessee. She graduated from O'More College of Design, in 2014, with her BFA. She has designed two collections, one of which was selected to be photographed by the O'More Research Academy. Her illustrations are published in *Join Me for Afternoon Tea*, *ABCs of Etiquette for Young People*, and *Live the Blessing*, the latter book featuring her art on the front cover. You can find more of her work at www.rehannagrant.wix.com/portfolio and www.etsy.com/shop/maeandaugust.

ABOUT THE AUTHOR

Jessa R. Sexton is a write-at-home mom, former professor, current homeschool teacher, and crafting enthusiast. A published author, her book list is below in a clean, bulleted format for your reading ease. She and her husband Jay love spending time with and talking about their children (Jack, Jonas, and June—yes, they all have "J" names, which was an accident at first and unavoidable after that), traveling, eating at new restaurants, and watching comedies. When Jessa experiences a rare moment alone, she watches classic television, composes songs and sonnets, reads, or gets lost in planning and goal setting.

- *Saturday*
- *Rose-Pie*
- *Eldy and Ohi*
- *With Your Fresh Thoughts*
- *MoBert's Irish Experience*
- *Live the Blessing*
- *These Things I Pray for You: My Child*
- *Educational Wellness* (co-written with Dr. K. Mark Hilliard)
- *Proverbs through the Generations* (co-written with Jack Hilliard and Dr. K. Mark Hilliard)